The Blow Off

by

Mickey J. Corrigan

The Blow Off

Contact Information: info@thewildrosepress.com

Cover Art by *Diana Carlile*

The Wild Rose Press, Inc.
PO Box 708
Adams Basin, NY 14410-0708

Visit us at www.thewildrosepress.com

Publishing History
First Mainstream Mystery Edition, 2015
Print ISBN 978-1-5092-0103-7
Digital ISBN 978-1-5092-0104-4

Published in the United States of America

Sometimes a girl has to take a guy for all he's got...

Angling out of the space, I poked my square nose into the bustle of evening commuter chaos. I was imagining what my girl gang would be like. We'd be smart vixens, a bunch of super-cool, daringly spicy, wildly tempting babes. Girls who could convince any guy in the toniest club to take them home for some one-on-one time, or some double-the-fun. Girls who would casually slip a man a tongue, a hand job, a mickey, then strip his room, his safe, his jewelry box. Take him on, then take him for all he was worth.

Boylston Street was more clogged than a fat man's arteries. Before I got to the atrial congestion on Mass. Ave., I banged a left, taking the back route home by all the crummy Northeastern University student dorms. Those buildings were in my past now. I'd earn the doctorate in education eventually, but on my own terms. No more sleeping on an air mattress on the floor with the other poor grad students. But no more fifty dollar blowjobs, either. I was going to ride the wave of girl-on-man crime. A budding entrepreneur, I'd grow my stable of foxy cons until we'd taken over the city of Boston. One wealthy sucker at a time.

I was so excited I sang *Happy Birthday* in a breathy voice all the way up Huntington Ave. to the VA hospital, where the traffic finally unclotted with a bloody burst and thinned out to a healthy trickle. I'd given myself a gift, a new moniker, and it was a perfect fit. Heaven Scent was now the handler of a beautiful, ballsy, all-female crew. I laughed. What's not to like about that job description?

While I waited at a red light in downbeat, trashy, but tree-lined Jamaica Plain, I was in the best mood I'd been in since my mother got married. I felt that same sense of freedom wash over me. I was fully independent, relieved of the burden of pleasing someone else. I had my own business! And soon, all my loan troubles would be behind me.

That was the dream, anyway.

PRAISE FOR AUTHOR

Mickey J. Corrigan

"For many readers, chick lit is like a comfy, well-worn security blanket. When you've had a long day and you just need to relax and unwind, it's familiar and undemanding...But author Mickey J. Corrigan spices up the same old short romance with a fun pulp fiction twist...quite possibly the best short e-book I've read in years."

~Nights and Weekends

"I've only read three of her books and she is HILARIOUS! I know I will be highly entertained by her shenanigans."

~Smardy Pants Book Blog

"There is nothing more thrilling to me than finding a writer whose work I can instantly fall in love with. Mickey J. Corrigan is one of those authors for me."

~Romance Junkies

"Mickey J. Corrigan's work isn't so much a contemporary romance as a sexy thriller. This is a writer who isn't so much interested in the 'nice' side of life, her characters tend to walk on the wild side and on the darker side of romance. But her stories are oh-so-compulsive all the same."

~Contemporary Romance Reviews

"It's official. I am in love with Mickey J. Corrigan. Her writing style is all her own and I cannot get enough of it. I love when she pulls me away from my life and shows me a dirty and different world like the towns she has created in South Florida. She gives me characters I shouldn't like with personalities no one would find endearing and makes me want to sit down and have a drink with them... There is no sugarcoating in a MJC book. Life is tough, but life is still good."

~For the Love of Books and Alcohol

Dedication

To Boston, my hometown and
the site of many crimes of passion and despair.

"My work is a lifelong celebration of futility."
                    –Roman Muradov, artist

Chapter One

My woman of the night career did not get off to a good start, so I decided to diversify. Entrepreneurship, the new black. Since I sucked at sucking dick, I formed a girl gang to seduce and rob rich johns. That was me, being creative and making the best of a badass situation. That's how my crew got started, anyway.

I never would have branched out except the hooker gig was an epic fail from day one. I just didn't have the chops. And you need chops. Most johns want fast head, that's all they're willing to go for these days. Nobody wants to catch a nasty STD, and time is of the essence when you're in a back alley or a parked car. I'm almost six feet tall. I wasn't designed for doing gymnastics in the musty darkness of a leatherette bucket seat.

After the first few hours of the ho routine, my lips went numb. My tongue was totally worn out. It's a muscle, the tongue, and mine had cramps. My chin needed a rest. I had a crick in my neck that wouldn't uncrick. And it was only my first night on the job.

Why oh why did you take out that loan for grad school, Shea O'Grady, I scolded myself as I manhandled yet another slack-dicked stranger. We were in an empty parking lot near MIT, squished into his Ford Escort. The car sucked as much as I did. Why was I always making the wrong decisions? I should have accepted the job offer I'd received from the

Jacksonville public school system, given up my silly dream of becoming a college professor in Boston. What was wrong with me?

As I worked my magic for the brief moment it took to ignite the animal flame inside yet another average chump, a guy too lazy or too stupid or too fucked up to have sex with a loved one, I thought about the mistakes of my life. I'd barely begun to make a mental list when my tenth john of the night exploded with a guttural caveman grunt.

They all sounded alike. Men, getting their rocks off. The more you pitched in to help, the more humdrum it became. I was twenty-five. Was this attitude of mine just a symptom of millennial generation malaise? Or did my day-to-day ennui already include sex? That would be tragic. I hoped the root cause was something else, like my new role as a cheap whore. Or maybe I wasn't cut out for this. Working for The Man. Maybe all sex workers felt like this. How could you like sex when somebody else was hogging the profits?

My musings were interrupted when Mr. John, an overweight businessman in a navy wool suit at least one size too small, grabbed me by the hair. Wow, that hurt. He shoved my head away from his generous lap with a brief review of my work. "Stupid bitch."

Ouch. Muthafuckah, as they say in Boston.

I sat up, said nothing to fat John. Instead, I flashed him an awkward grin. My neck was killing me. Time to cash out for the night, head for the Epsom salts. Outside the dirty windows of the dirty Ford, rain had begun to fall. Buckets of dirty rain. The perfect end to a perfect evening.

It was later, while soaking my neck—and the rest of my body, which felt cold from walking too far in the rain and sore from the heavy paws of strangers—that I suddenly realized exactly how I might deviate from the daily grind. Sitting in the steamy bath, a Heineken in one hand, a tweezered joint in the other, the idea came to me. Fully formed. There it was—a brilliant business plan. A better way to use my skills and youth and looks. I was in hot water up to my chin. Why not add more?

To be honest, I'm not a gorgeous chick. But I am relatively attractive—shiny auburn hair, long legs, and a nice set of perky tits. And I'm practical. So I knew my sex object status was only a temporary window in the long life of a very average woman. Why waste the brief period of seductiveness I'd been given? Wasn't it my god-given right to capitalize on my temporary allure?

Hooking was certainly one way to cash in, but as I had just discovered, not a satisfying one. I wasn't good at it. I doubted I'd get better. My heart wasn't in it. Neither was the rest of my body, apparently. Plus, sex for pay was going to mess up my libido. Hardly seemed worth the aggravation. I massaged my tender neck.

I sucked some good green smoke into my lungs, held my breath, and thought of a better way to use sex appeal to pay my bills. Instantly, I was pumped. My new business idea could relieve me of the burden of nightly blowjobs. I'm no actress. I can look comatose when I'm not mentally engaged in something that interests me. But with a variation on the job description, one that required more intellectual engagement and less drudgery, I might be able to work the gig longer than a single, painful night.

Exhaling a stream of green and feeling so much

3

better, I had to smile. I now knew what I needed from the whoring biz. I needed to be my own boss. With a crew. Working for me.

Wow. I had leadership aspirations! Who knew?

I snuffed out the joint and polished off the beer. Why work for The Man when you could *be* The Man? Smokey Robinson supposedly said that to Berry Gordy, who went on to found the Motown Record empire. Love that retro music. Those girl groups were killer.

Not too much later, I crawled into bed and, listening to the steady slam of rain against the windows, I drifted off to sleep. I slept well that night and got up refreshed. The sun was streaming in, the blue jays calling out to warn the earthworms of their impending doom. Nature can be so thoughtful.

I brewed up an extra strong pot of coffee. All day, I worked on my business plan.

That night, the second and last of my hooker career, I went to see Cedrick7Z with a business proposition. I was nervous, so I underdressed. Red silk hot pants, white lace bustier, lots of clunky gold, and five-inch do-me pumps with fiberglass heels.

My handler lounged in his usual spot at the John Hancock Jazz Bar, nursing a blue martini. With a strength of purpose and a vibrant confidence I didn't really feel, I slinkied up to the faux leather booth in a dark corner of the softly lit barroom. Then I stood there, heart whirring, until he finally looked up at me.

His black eyes narrowed, pinning me against an invisible wall. I stared back, breathless.

To my relief, the down tempo music helped a little, smoothing out my edginess. Which was essential because Cedrick7Z was going to be a challenge. The

Man was impatient with women. He was also an egomaniac with a notoriously vicious temper. Fortunately for me, my handler had a couple standards. He never fucked around with his sex workers once he'd hired them, and he paid us a competitive twenty-five percent on individual take.

I had to admire the guy. A combination of animal instinct and street smarts had helped launch him from scuzzy gangbanger to pimp alpha dog. In certain parts of Boston—not the nice parts, of course, but the busy and ever-popular scum districts—Cedrick7Z was a powerful man. A man to be respected. And feared.

I gave him a sexy pout and puffed out my chest. Like a robin getting ready to sing for a mate. My heart calmed itself off the ledge with some internal words of reassurance. What was the worst that could happen? The Man would not like my business idea and would order me to go back to playing the skin flute.

"What you want, girl?" Cedrick7Z said, a scowl darkening his baggy, hound-dog face. Your generic pimp, he was duded up in a mint green sateen jacket, signature black leather gloves, and a white angora turtleneck. Two gold hoops dangled from his right ear. "You s'posed to be on the Internet, lookin' for dick."

It was risky, but I made my move. With a quick nod of my head, I sat down directly across from him. I'd worn my hair down, and I let it tumble like autumn leaves around my bare shoulders. He glanced at my cleavage, squeezed just so by my tight top. I licked my thickly glossed lips, fluttered my black paste-on lashes.

When I was sure Cedrick7Z saw just how seductive I could be, I said in my R-rated movie trailer voice, "I have a better idea for what we could do to capitalize on my talents. Give me a few minutes of your time, I think you'll agree with me." I waited until he nodded, then I said, "I have three words for you—seduce and rob."

He grinned. "Go on, baby. I'm listenin'."

Ten minutes later, I had my own blue martini sitting on the white linen tablecloth in front of us. And I was on the verge of sealing a verbal with my handler.

"I like it," he said with a disorienting flash of white and gold teeth. He leaned in, touched my hand. His raccoon eyes showed the whites all around. "But you got to get your own stable, girl, not me. You find the johns you'sef. And you don't let your doin's touch my business. You do all dat, I say, have at it, babe."

He had a good thing going with the local barmen, club bouncers, hotel concierges, and the area cops. He didn't need any bad press to taint his street rep. I totally got that.

When I reached for my drink, he gripped my hand. Hard. *Ouch.*

"I get fitty percent all earnings. Take come straight to me. You and your girls get your pull *after* the merchandise appraised by my guy. Got that, pussycake?"

When I nodded, he let go of my hand. I used my other hand to lift my glass to my slightly trembling lips. I sipped my drink. Oh, that Bombay Sapphire was nice. It had been some time since I'd enjoyed an expensive cocktail.

Smiling now, I said, "If we're going to be business partners, I'd prefer it if you would call me by my stage name. Heaven Scent. Or Ms. Scent, if you're feeling formal."

6

Cedrick7Z laughed. His gold teeth outnumbered the white ones. "You amuse me, girl. Now get outta here. Go make me some money."

I downed the rest of the martini and licked my lips. Ah, that hit the spot. There would be more of those in my future. My very near future.

Still smiling, I stood up and leaned over my pimp. He smelled like juniper berries and baked potato, not an unpleasant combination. My long thin arm looked especially pale when I wrapped it around his thick, black neck.

"I will make you happy you believed in me," I whispered in his unadorned ear. "Who says men and women can't play on the same team and both win?"

He pulled away, gave me a nasty scowl. "You don't bring me some serious bling by Saturday, it be back to suckin' dick for you, baby. Now go on. I got other business to tend to."

When I fluttered my hand in a queenish wave goodbye, Cedrick7Z just stared at me blankly. I sashayed out of Nectar's as slowly and Marilyn Monroe-ishly as I could.

As soon as I hit the sidewalk, though, I shed my killer heels. Clutching them in one hand, I ran barefoot the four blocks to my car. Shit, man, I had to get a move on. I needed to round up a team to assist me. Pronto. I had to build a crew of hot looking, racy girls. Girls with guts and brains, girls with diamonds in their eyes and a driving urge to take others' tender for themselves. I would have to find two, three, maybe four young women willing and able to take the risk, women who would trust one another enough to form a girl gang. Women who really wanted—needed—and were desperate enough to do this kind of dirty work. They would have to want it as much as I did.

And they had to be available. Right now. Because we had less than five days to pull off our first sexy heist.

The night was overcast but blessedly dry. And warm. Too warm for early June. It was going to be a hot summer in the city. While I unlocked the car, I sniffed at the air. Yum. The magnolias on Comm. Ave. were in bloom. I'd always loved those flowers, their pearly little petals, the gush of sweet scent. Made Boston smell like the long sweet springtimes of the south, of home.

When I gunned the engine, the Mini issued its tiny mouse roar. Laughable. The 1977 vintage automobile sounded like a kid's toy, a joke. But it got me from here to there whenever I was dressed inappropriately for public transportation. Which was becoming more and more the case.

I put her in gear and waited for a break in the traffic, which was incessant and loud.

After my ex-boyfriend went walkabout in Australia and failed to return, I'd kept his car keys, among other items he left behind. The Mini was fun—forest green with racecar stripes and a lot of pep. It was badder than it sounded. The little Britmobile got great gas mileage and was incredibly reliable. In fact, Mini and me got along better than Antoine and I ever had.

Angling out of the space, I poked my square nose into the bustle of evening commuter chaos. I was imagining what my girl gang would be like. We'd be smart vixens, a bunch of super-cool, daringly spicy, wildly tempting babes. Girls who could convince any guy in the toniest club to take them home for some one-on-one time, or some double-the-fun. Girls who would casually slip a man a tongue, a hand job, a mickey, then strip his room, his safe, his jewelry box. Take him on, then take him for all he was worth.

Boylston Street was more clogged than a fat man's arteries. Before I got to the atrial congestion on Mass. Ave., I banged a left, taking the back route home by all the crummy Northeastern University student dorms. Those buildings were in my past now. I'd earn the doctorate in education eventually, but on my own terms. No more sleeping on an air mattress on the floor with the other poor grad students. But no more fifty dollar blowjobs, either. I was going to ride the wave of girl-on-man crime. A budding entrepreneur, I'd grow my stable of foxy cons until we'd taken over the city of Boston. One wealthy sucker at a time.

I was so excited I sang *Happy Birthday* in a breathy voice all the way up Huntington Ave. to the VA hospital, where the traffic finally unclotted with a bloody burst and thinned out to a healthy trickle. I'd given myself a gift, a new moniker, and it was a perfect fit. Heaven Scent was now the handler of a beautiful, ballsy, all-female crew. I laughed. What's not to like about that job description?

While I waited at a red light in downbeat, trashy, but tree-lined Jamaica Plain, I was in the best mood I'd been in since my mother got married. I felt that same sense of freedom wash over me. I was fully independent, relieved of the burden of pleasing someone else. I had my own business! And soon, all my loan troubles would be behind me.

That was the dream, anyway.

Chapter Two

My street had no available parking spaces, and I wasn't in the mood to traipse around the iffy neighborhood in my sleaze outfit. So I drove around the block.

Working in the underground marketplace had never been a goal of mine. My future plans had centered around the attainment of academic success— scoring top grades in the notoriously lousy Florida public schools, attending a good college steeped in the academic tea party that is Boston, getting accepted at a decent university for graduate school. I didn't have my eye on business school, law school, or one of the shark tanks on Wall Street. I was so idealistic, so squeaky clean, I actually wanted to teach kids about literature.

So why did I become a hooker? Could it have been the subtle and not so subtle influence during my formative years of my slutty any-guy-will-do mother?

This was the reason I gave myself, for a while at least. That, and today's loan-heavy economy. Carrying too much college debt? Too busy with my education to fit in a nine-to-five job? Why not become a sugar baby, a rich man's toy, a streetwalker? Lie back, relax, and let sex-starved men solve my personal financial problems.

An abundance of desperate guys were out there, cruising the Internet or the dark city streets, looking to hand over cash for release. I liked to think of whoring as a catch and release program. Like fishing. And there were plenty of fish in the triple-X sea. A lot of needy men, poking around dirty dating sites or driving around in their late model sedans. Walking the beat in the theatre district, hands shoved deep in their pockets, furtive eyes on the young girls in netted stockings.

I crawled around the block a second time. No parking spaces were available anywhere near my apartment building. A typical Monday night. What could I do? I drove around the block yet again. And again. I loved Jamaica Plain in the summer. Most of the students left town, and the artsy neighborhood opened its arms to the year-round residents. We'd hang together at the pubs, drinking discount beers and catching up on who's sleeping with who. Or walk the pond and watch the itty-bitty sailboats try to trap some wind. I usually spent weekend mornings at the Arboretum, reading and dozing under the lush green canopies of unusual trees from around the world. If I hadn't been so broke, I would've bought myself a condo and stayed for the rest of my life. But parking was always a problem, and if you lived here, you dealt with it.

When a battered Saab pulled out of a tight spot, I scooted in. I had to jimmy my little car into the sliver of a space that had magically appeared right in front of my red brick, World War II era apartment building. Hopefully, nobody would steal my battery tonight. I was tired of replacing it. Why me and my battery? The petty thieves always seemed to target me. Maybe that was why I was motivated to become one of them. Return the favor, but ratchet it up a bunch of notches.

I locked the car and hurried up the crackled

sidewalk to the crumbling front steps, fuck-me shoes in hand. My mind was clicking though all the girls I knew, attempting to think of one who might be up for rape-drugging and plundering men. My mental tally was stuck on the sole candidate—me.

As soon as I pushed through the front door and stepped into the empty lobby, I could smell the sweet intoxication of medical marijuana. Buck, the building manager, was obviously self-medicating again.

Buck.

Quickly, I hopped into my shoes and patted my hair down, primping a little in the glass reflection from the front door. Then I hustled down the dank hallway to the manager's office.

Buck. But of course! My good pal Buck could help me with my new business. The man knew everyone in our four-story building and an awful lot of other folks around town. Notably the shadier characters. And more than his fair share of attractive women. I'd seen them come and go. I already had a couple in mind, a sexy orange-haired chick and a super tall—taller than me, even—black woman who looked like a model for athletic fashion.

Behind the oak door with the pseudo-brass *Manager* sign, Bob Marley was wailing about no women. From what I understood, he had plenty of women. As did Buck.

I rapped several times before I heard Rascal "Buck" Bearman shuffling to the other side of the door. How many Rastafarian types are named Buck? Probably just the one, and he was quite the individual. I'd never met anyone so uniquely unsuited to his name and, for that matter, current occupation.

"What's this for?" Buck said, his voice a smoker's gruff growl.

My heart sped up. Buck had this sexy way of talking that made everything sound like a big cat's purr.

"It's me, Shea. I need to talk to you," I said, using my breathy, Heaven Scent accent. Buck and I were friends, but sometimes I donned the seductive persona. Usually when the rent was overdue. "Not about the rent, either," I added in order to clarify.

The door locks clicked open. "I'm in the middle of a batch. C'mon back to the kitchen."

He left the door open a crack. I pushed it wide enough to let myself in. The smell of pot was overpowering, but it blended with another aroma. Chocolate, semisweet chocolate. My mouth watered a little. Dinner had consisted of soba ramen flavored with a packet of miso soup. Grad school diet—cold cereal in the morning, coffee all day, freeze-dried glop for supper. My stomach growled as I made my way past the bongo drums, cardboard boxes, and wooden crates that spilled from every corner of the dusty, twenty-by-twenty room.

"Smells good," I hinted when I reached the brightly lit back end of Buck's studio apartment.

"New recipe. I'm improvising." Buck's chest bulged from a thin white tank, wide and furry as a bear rug. The man had perfect pecs. His caramel-colored arms were cut, nicely muscled, and his golden brown dreadlocks hung down his broad back like a mane. He was quite the hottie.

He turned around and bent over the beat-up stove, flashing me his cute ass crack while retrieving something from the hot oven. Wafts of sweet brownie aroma hit me like a childhood memory would've if I'd had a mother who could bake. I didn't have that luxury, but my olfactory nerves still got jazzed.

I took a deep breath, savoring it. "Yum. Need any sampling performed?"

Buck snorted. "Do I ask you that about your products?" When he turned to me again, he was gripping a restaurant-size pan of chronic brownies with bulky blue oven mitts. "But I might trade you a bit of this for a bit of that."

He was kidding, of course. I'd told him about my last ditch bid to make enough money to pay off the circling college loan sharks. Buck didn't exactly encourage me to go a-hoing, but he didn't try to talk me out of it either. He was that good a friend.

"You enjoy your first day at the new job? How're the knees?" he asked.

I shrugged. "Work blows," I joked lamely.

Neither of us laughed. His dark eyes took all of me in, sucked me right down like a black hole might do. He had a crush on me, and we both knew it. But I wasn't going there. I liked him too much to take him for a pony ride. I saved that for my less favorite men. And now, apparently, for total strangers.

I pulled up a rickety wicker bar stool and sat down at the white tile snack bar. "Look, Buck, I have a serious proposition for you. Let me lick the pan when you're done with it, and I'll cut you in on something. Potentially lucrative for all parties."

"Except the wronged parties, I assume."

He found a long, thin knife in a drawer and, setting the pan on the counter between us, proceeded to cut the brownies into perfect squares. His lips, held still in deep concentration, were pink, soft, and wet. His body, on full display before me, was bulky, big, and hard. Ooh. The guy was a hunk of man meat.

I, however, was vegetarian.

"I'm listening," he said.

I inhaled deeply. Boy, that chocolate smelled delicious. So did Buck. I had to reel in my thoughts. Was I getting stoned just sitting there, breathing the air of his apartment? Wouldn't be the first time I'd ended up with a contact high simply from being around Buck.

"Here's the thing," I told him. "I gave it my all last night. All of about four hours. But I hate hooking. It's dull. Same old, same old, suck, suck, sucks, you know? So I thought up a way to make it more entertaining. And more profitable." I paused until he looked up, then gave him my most alluring smile. "But I'll need your help."

Buck went back to transferring the brownies one at a time into small plastic sandwich bags. Not a crumb to be spared. He knew how to preserve the integrity of each single-serving high. I doubted there would be any leftovers in the baking pan for me to snarf up.

"One night on the street, and it's on to other professions?" He shook his handsome head, clucking. "Too bad, Shea. I thought you had more stamina than that."

I punched his bulging bicep lightly, and he stiffened. "Don't make me drop one of these high-test babies. They're solid shit, man."

"Sorry. But don't you want to hear what my new business is?"

"No." No? How could that be? How could Buck turn me down? He didn't even know what I was proposing. Plus, the guy liked me, we were good friends and neighbors, and he was always looking for ways to make more money. His brief stint at Berkeley College of Music had left him with insurmountable debt.

He talked about it all the time, complaining how he couldn't afford to play gigs in the rock clubs anymore. He needed to move product, which was a far more profitable use of his time. That's how he'd ended up full-time in the dope biz. Oh, Buck had adapted, he was doing okay. But I knew how much he resented the idea that the business model had been forced on him. He had to keep playing supplier if he ever wanted to get the government loan monkey off his back.

He sealed up a baggie with a swift slide of his long, drummer's fingers. "Can't help you. Sorry, Shea, I don't do blowjobs. Even for money."

"Funny. But hey, neither do I. Not anymore. As for you, Bucko, what I meant was, I need you to help me find women who will. Or women who can act like they will. See, I'm putting together a crew," I explained. "I've been promoted to handler."

"Handler for what? Kink? F on F? *Fifty Shades*, all that shit?"

His hands worked quickly, sealing up the little bags. Buck had real nice hands, with smooth almond-colored skin and clipped white nails. I wouldn't say no to those hands, if things were different. But they weren't. Things in my sorry life were ever the fucking same.

"Girl gang, not kink. I'm going to put together a crack team. A crew of attractive, sexy, smart seductresses who can spot a mark, convince him to take them home, then drug him up and take what he's got. An X-rated bling ring for naughty adults."

He didn't comment, just handed me an unsealed baggie. I almost had an orgasm. I'm not sure what turned me on more, his large warm hand on mine or the idea of eating one of his supercharged brownies.

While I sniffed inside the bag and made animal noises, Buck watched me. He didn't laugh.

"This is serious stuff, Shea. You can face some very stiff charges with this gig. They won't let you off with a wink and a BJ, either. You get caught ripping off your johns, you'll score yourself a hefty sentence."

I took a small bite of the pot brownie. "Oh, my god, Buck. Yum fucking yum. You stuffed them with peanut butter? Wow." I gobbled it down in three piggish bites.

"Somebody had ramen for dinner. Again," he teased. "Seriously, you willing to take a chance on going to prison? I, for one, can vouch for the bad food, scratchy linens, and unpleasant company."

Buck had done a stint for possession with intent to sell. Six months in Concord. He rarely discussed it. The whole thing embarrassed him. His father was a dentist, his mom a school principal. He'd had a cleaner upbringing than I had, but we'd both ended up in the shit.

"Not to mention, your darling pimp. Cedrick the Entertainer isn't going to let you rip off his paying customers, Shea."

I giggled. The weed was almost as good as the brownie. My mind was drifting nicely, and I didn't even try to follow it. But I managed to explain Cedrick7Z's angle. "I find the marks, and I manage my own crew. He's in for fifty percent because he sells off the loot to a fence."

"The pimp is in? Interesting," Buck mused. "'If the pay's right and it's legal, he'll do it. If the pay's right, he'll do it.'"

He was quoting lines from a film by the Coen Brothers, who I loved as well, so I laughed. Buck grinned, then turned around to reach into the refrigerator for a couple of long necks. His ass was adorable, furry crack and all. I admired it, wondering what he would be like in bed. Oops, guess I was already high. My judgment was always the first to fade. Muscle control would be next.

After popping off the caps, Buck handed me a cold bottle of Bud. I took a long swig while he settled onto the stool next to me. For a moment, I stared at his muscular thighs encased in a pair of pale, ripped jeans. I had to force myself to stop ogling.

Buck didn't seem to notice. He sipped his beer. "Sounds like you have it all worked out. So what do you need me for, Shea?"

I belched. Ripe, resonant. Buck smiled, tolerant, mildly amused. He really did like the real me. Vulgarity and all.

"I need you to recommend some fine women," I told him. "Good-looking, bold, tough. Women in need of work. Women with balls of fire. Fiery, bold, balled women." I suddenly laughed uproariously. Totally baked, all right. I'm such a cheap date. I stopped laughing long enough to add, "Not baldheaded, but ballsy. You know what I mean."

Buck was watching me intently. His thigh rested against mine. He smelled smoky and sweet, like hickory barbecue.

"You have girlfriends like that?" I asked him. "Smart women sick of their dead-end jobs? Good women who've been jilted, women with overdue bills and college loans up the yin-yang? What about women who just want to make some serious cash off some seriously lame rich guys?"

"Every woman I know needs money real bad right now. And I mean regular chicks, nice women, not pros. But they're open to alternatives because they're desperate. Like us." His eyes cast up to the ceiling, thinking, probably, about all the women he knew. Which had to be dozens, possibly hundreds. Men as hunky as Buck tended to know a lot of women.

After a moment, he said, "If I wanted to, I could get you as many girls as you need."

I laughed again, but Buck didn't. He looked at me, unsmiling, and sipped his beer. He wasn't joking around.

So I sobered up, or tried to. Boy, that weed was strong. My neck was totally cured of its crick, and my limbs felt like they were made out of warm saltwater taffy.

"Well, I like the girl with the orange hair. And the really tall, African-looking girl," I said to Buck. He gave me a weird look, so I added, "I see them in the lobby, or out front, waiting for you to buzz them in. Hey, I'm not judging. They look like terrific chicks."

He snorted, then picked up his smart phone and started pressing keys. "I'll make some connections for you, then I'm out. Just doing a favor for a friend. Okay?"

While I sat there next to Buck in his hot kitchen,

pumped and lusty and somewhat fried, he locked in a meeting with four of his female friends. For ten o'clock.

When he hung up on the last of them, it was nine-forty-five.

Chapter Three

Ginger, Mary-Ann, Skipper and Mrs. Howl. These were the names I chose for my new crew. I kept my hooker moniker, Heaven Scent, and nicknamed Buck "Mr. B." You don't want to use your real names when you work in the underground. It's better to call one another by your stage names. You need to get used to your own alias, let it become you. Or you become it.

This would be my first bit of advice as handler. My own handler would not be advising my crew. I was the only crew member who would meet with Cedrick7Z.

Before the girls arrived for the audition, I called my former pimp. He reminded me about keeping him out of it, saying again how he had to remain at a distance from my crew. And he insisted on anonymity. "I'll take on your take, girl. Otherwise, I'm at large from your illegal activity. No B&E, kidnappin', any of that shit charge for me. So, this is the deal—you the middleman. Don't even talk about me, hear? That way, your pussies don't got nuthin' they'd use to squeal on me, they ever get in a pinch and seek out some leverage."

I agreed to his demands. What choice did I have? But his CYA attitude annoyed me. Who did he think he was? As if pimping were legal. As if what we were doing wasn't just the logical extension of what *he* was doing.

But I didn't have time to worry about it. The girls began to arrive at Buck's apartment in quick, lovely succession.

Creating the crew turned out to be easy, because Buck had exceptional taste in women. Attractive, alluring women with simple but serious problems only fast money could solve. Still, I chose my gang carefully. Sure, I was stoned, but the weed expanded my mind and provided me with keener senses, sharper intuition.

Or so I told myself.

All four of the women who agreed to drop by Buck's on short notice passed the desirability test with flying colors, each one a hot babe in her own special way. Cute, sexy, smart. They were young, they were willing, they all claimed to have what it would take to seduce and rob. Only one of the four seemed a little uptight when I discussed the finer points of seduction as foreplay to grand theft.

"I don't know, this sounds kinda dangerous," Mrs. Howl said, flipping her bleach blonde hair over one bare shoulder.

She sat on the couch with one of the other girls while the rest of us sprawled on the dusty hardwood floor. Buck had gone down the street for a beer, leaving us to work out the details. I sneezed. The man needed a cleaning lady. Bad.

"What if we run into them again afterward? And they recognize us?" Mrs. Howl's amber eyes were wide, and her small hands played nervously with the hem of her green rayon shift.

"That's a chance we'll have to take," I said. "But

you can be reassured these johns won't report us. Because if they do, they'll be admitting to getting conned. By a broad. A bimbo they picked up in a bar, no less. No man wants to admit something like that. No guy likes to have other guys find out he got played by a female. And many of these men will have wives, girlfriends, fiancés. Jobs and reputations. It's foolproof that way."

She shrugged and looked away. The girl was skeptical. Beautiful as she might be, her lack of confidence would never fly in the quick con business.

I sent the nervous blonde out to the all-night convenience store on the corner for espressos. Then the rest of us bonded over kicking Mrs. Howl off the island. Like the contestants on those cheesy reality shows always seem to do.

"She's got cold feet now, she'll never be able to drug some horny man," Ginger said, tossing her wild frazzle of carrot-colored curls. She sat next to me, her thin legs crossed in the lotus position. Flexible, long-limbed, she looked like the hippie yoga sort of chick who lives in communes and digs vegan food. "We need to be able to rely on one another to come through, do the job."

Mary-Ann, a pixie-faced beauty with a heavy Boston accent, agreed. "Never taken money for sex before. But I *have* stolen stuff from guys. Guys I dated. And it takes a certain coldness. To get up out of bed and do that. Not sure the chick has that kind of edge." She pushed her dark bangs out of her big round eyes and shrugged. Mary-Ann was tough, street-smart, and sharp-tongued. I liked her shoot-from-the-hip style.

"What sort of stuff did you steal?" Skipper asked,

one thin eyebrow cocked. An Amazonian with a waist-length waterfall of hair and skin the color of *café au lait*, she was both striking and strong-minded. Nothing like the fat oaf captain on the TV series, but she did have an imposing size and a catchy laugh. I liked her instantly. She gave a mean handshake, unlike a lot of women. She also asked good questions and listened carefully to the answers. Skipper was planning to become a psychotherapist, but at the moment she was taking a break from college and driving cab. She'd be terrific at both jobs, no doubt, but a waste of talent and beauty in either profession.

Mary-Ann ran a small hand through her glossy hair. "Watches, cash, expensive bottles of wine. Stamps, coins, baseball cards. Not that much, really. And only when I felt like they owed me. Especially the cheap guys, the losers in bed. Orgasm deadbeats who expect head and don't return the favor." She rolled her eyes. "Never got caught either."

"And that's the plan here as well," I interjected. "To never get caught."

"I'm not fucking these guys," Skipper said. "I'll rock their boats, but I'm not going all the way in. Staying dry. That okay?"

When the other two made murmurs of agreement, I said, "Course not. The key is going to be to knock them out before they get you under the sheets. Every time, that's how we'll want the game to play out."

"Okay, then count me in. But I think we need to keep it to just us four," Skipper said. "And let Mrs. Howl go. Just to be safe."

The rest of us nodded. We were thinking like a team already.

By midnight, our castoff had gone back to her house share in Revere while the rest of us moved the meeting to the corner bar. I loved Señor Cancun's. Sleazy, low-rent, tacky. And reveling in its own low-brow insignificance. The perfect hangout.

Buck joined us as I ordered a pitcher of the house sangria and instructed Jerry to put it on my tab. The red-headed bartender was into bartered trade. I didn't mind. I'd known Jerry since I'd moved to town, and he was a mighty fine lay. Neither of us was looking for something permanent. Just a way to let off steam once in a while.

After setting the fruity wine on our table, Jerry winked at me and mouthed the word, "One." As in, "I get off at one a.m., so be ready to roll." I smiled at him, and he strutted off. He had a footballer's back and a butt that made any pair of jeans look good. I let my eyes linger.

When I turned back to the crew, I caught Buck staring at me with a strange, uneasy expression. He had brownie crumbs stuck to the bristles on his chin. I winked, but he didn't acknowledge it. I wasn't sure why he would care if I banged the bartender since he himself had slept with all of the women at our table. Except me. Besides, he knew I was a hooker. A retired hooker turned seductress grifter. The handler of a female con crew. So really, what did he expect?

I frowned at him until he looked away. Then I poured everyone a full glass of sweet red wine. "To the triple X bling ring."

We raised our wine glasses and clinked them together.

Buck held back. "I'm just the headhunter. Like

always, I'm nothing but the supplier. You girls are on your own with this thing." He ignored the wine and worked on his bottle of Bud.

"You'll be sorry when we're rockin' and rollin' the fat dogs," I told him.

He didn't respond, but he did give me a long, heated stare. Oo-la-la, the guy smoldered. I shivered a little, drank my sangria.

****

Buck left early with Ginger in tow. They made a cute couple, but I planned to advise him that, after tonight, he'd need to keep his hands off my crew. I didn't want anybody falling in love and retiring prematurely. Not before we had a chance to make us some serious money. I needed my girls to be focused, always fresh, on the ready to lure and rob. They needed to be on call with no strings attached.

With the token male gone, our chatter turned to men, money, and family. The usual girl talk. The three of us had a lot in common. No serious boyfriends. Oversize debt that came from nowhere and bills that piled up faster than we could pay them down. And we were all close to our families. Maybe too close for women in their twenties.

Skipper picked a soggy green grape from her glass of sangria and popped it in her mouth. "My dad would kill me if he knew what kind of side job I was taking on. He's a desk cop. In Brewster."

"Will he be a problem?" I asked. "I mean, will he investigate the source of your income stream once the flow suddenly increases?"

Skipper snickered. "Nah. He's got a new girlfriend, and she's expecting. He's too busy with his own life to worry about mine." She shook her head, her thick hair tumbling about her wide, shapely shoulders. "Besides, I plan to bank and invest. Pay off my debts slowly, like any enterprising cabbie working overtime on the busy streets of Beantown. I'm not interested in drawing attention to myself."

But the girl couldn't help it. Inevitably, she was the center of attention. Because of her unusual size and beauty, everywhere she went people took notice. She couldn't avoid being the focus of more than her share of male interest.

I glanced around the crowded bar. Two middle-aged drunks sat facing us on their stools, backs to the bar so they could stare our way. T-shirts stretched tight over basketball guts, the two white guys only had eyes for the tall, majestic black woman. Even though there was no band, no dance floor, each of them had already weaved over to our table to ask Skipper to dance. We'd laughed at them quietly as, one by one, the men approached and retreated. They took their slapdowns like gentlemen, accepting the expected verdict with sheepish grins. Maybe they'd made a bet with one another. Maybe she was just irresistible. I figured it was the latter.

After the drunks gave up, a table of businessmen in rumpled suits sent over a fresh pitcher of sangria. Which we were happy to accept. We'd been on the verge of ordering another round anyway. One of the group came by to see how we liked our drinks. He was sloppy drunk, sloppy fat, his jowls shaking when he talked. He stared at Skipper, then handed her his card, said to call him if she wanted any modeling work.

"Modeling his stumpy cock in my vagina, no

doubt," she said after he'd wandered back to his boys. "But hey. Ain't this sangria the best?"

Mary-Ann and I looked at one another and smiled. We had our charms, and we could seduce with the best of them. But Skipper? The woman was a dick magnet. A hot goddess.

This would work in our favor when we were out on the prowl. We'd be able to use Skipper to trawl for the richest men, the alpha dogs. Ginger and Mary-Ann could serve as backup, they'd handle the more mortal men on the hunt. I'd pinch hit, but mainly I would hang back. I'd be on the outside so I could call the shots and manage the con. That was the game plan, at least.

When Skipper headed off to the ladies room, I swear to god, every guy in the room watched her go by. You don't see women like that in Boston every day, certainly not in the dreary 'burbs or the rundown neighborhoods of Jamaica Plain. The girl would definitely be an asset to our crew, but I realized that, because she was so unique, she'd be awfully easy to ID. If it ever came to that.

The plan was for it never to come to that.

"Jaysus, that girl is something else," Mary-Ann said.

We smiled at one another.

I forged ahead. "So, what about you? Where are you from originally?"

"Right here," she told me.

But she didn't mean Señor Cancun's. Mary-Ann had grown up in nearby Dorchester, still lived at home in the family's triple-decker. A single mom by twenty-one, she had two kids under school age. I asked how she would juggle our night time excursions with her domestic duties.

Skipper slid back into the booth just as Mary-Ann said, "Thank god for my twin brother. He loves my boys."

"You have a twin?" Skipper asked, black eyes glittering. "I'd love to check him out. He must be adorable."

"Mark's cute, all right. But he's got issues. Came down with cancer when he was twenty. Chemo trashed him for a long while." Mary-Ann polished off her wine in a single gulp. "He's bouncing back now. Might even be able to get a job in another year or two. I pay him what I can to watch the boys while I'm chambermaiding or waitressing private parties. I pay some rent to the folks, too. But four years of humongous medical bills did in my parents. They're basically wiped out."

She looked at us, her eyes hard. "Fucking health care system. My parents work for the city, both of them. They've put in their time. Jaysus. You'd think the insurance they get from the government would cover everything. Not so. Not so."

Skipper poured more wine for each of us. Mary-Ann thanked her, then suddenly erupted. She spouted off for a while about the unfairness of her brother's illness, her parents' ensuing debt. "Fuck doing it by the book. You get screwed in the end if you're honest, hardworking, moral. You get fucked, and then where are you?"

I had to agree. "Life sucks if you play by the rules." I was thinking about my own decades of studying and schooling. The eternal sales pitch of hard work leading to career success looked nothing like the harsh reality of scrounging in garbage cans with your useless bachelor's degree in your torn back pocket. "So much of it is a con. By the government, the corporations, the education mafia. By the media, the frigging banks."

Skipper nodded. "My parents might not go along with that, but they both started earning money when they were in middle school, and eventually paid for college with their savings. They got jobs so easily, they have no idea how hard it is for us. Only loan my parents ever had was the mortgage on their little house in Brewster, which they got for a song. A freaking *song,* compared to housing prices nowadays. And they paid that off before the thirty years were even up."

She looked at us, blinked. "He's black, she's white. They had their shit to deal with back in the seventies. He traded her for a younger model a few years ago, but my mom's tough. She's fine. She's so busy now with her organic cosmetics business. They've done okay for themselves, despite everything. Neither of them ever had to whore themselves out like I do. Driving cab. Writing other students' papers for them. Now this."

She bit her bottom lip. We all had misgivings. But we all had motivations that were stronger than our hesitations. Bigger than our sense of morality. More powerful than the desire to stay out of trouble by playing by the rules.

I sipped my fruity wine. I had a pretty good buzz going. "I'm with you there, Skipper. Nobody wants to bend over for a living. But I'm not the only whore in my family. When I was a kid, my mom slept with every available guy in Jacksonville, and some of the unavailable ones." I let out a laugh, a scornful, joyless sound. "She made sure our rent was paid for that way. Sometimes, one of her men would take us in for a week or a month or two, and we'd eat family-style dinners at his rickety kitchen table. Big coup for my mom, mac and cheese on chipped Formica."

What a farce. Trailer parks, rundown apartment complexes, crappy developments surrounded by palmetto scrub. Everywhere cheap and ugly and hotter than hell.

"Until she hit the jackpot with Kent, her current husband," I continued. "Married into a wealthy family, and now she lives like royalty. In a big house in a fancy-ass gated community in St. Augustine." I smiled, but with something other than happiness. "I love her, and she deserves all she can get from this life. But I'll fuck with clowns and take their cash in a bid for my own life, rather than sell myself to a rich man for the rest of my days."

Skipper nodded enthusiastically. Her thickly lashed eyes glowed. When Mary-Ann piped up with "Right on, sistah," Skipper and I laughed.

"So where we gonna find our first—" Mary-Ann started to say, then stopped herself with a small smile.

Another businessman was approaching our table, drink in hand. Not the fat guy who'd offered modeling work, but a preppie sort in his early forties. Prematurely gray, sky-blue eyes, chiseled face. Handsome, if you like your men dipped in wax. He wavered a little, unsure. But he eventually got brave and walked right up to stand beside Skipper. She rolled her eyes at us and turned to face him as he hovered over our booth, a wealthy, well-dressed moon. We all waited for him to say something, but he just stood there, shining his nightlight on Skipper.

"Go ahead, Charlie," she said finally. "Hit me with your best shot."

He laughed, nervous. "Uh, okay. But the name's Wendell. Wendell Hawthorne. The, uh, third."

He cleared his throat, smoothed the back of his head with one manicured hand. His shimmery hair was slicked back, his Armani suit perfectly pressed. I peeked at his finger. No fuck-ring. But that didn't mean anything, not in a grunge-hole like Señor Cancun's.

"Um. I think you're a total knockout," he stammered. "How'd you like to go out to dinner some night? Just you and me?"

Mary-Ann harrumphed and I pouted. We were kidding, but Wendell didn't catch on. His eyes darted about. He was afraid to hear Skipper's answer. Afraid she'd say no, maybe more afraid she'd say yes. She was intimidating. Big, black, way too beautiful.

"There's this new seafood place down by the wharf…" he said.

While he stumbled through his pitch, I slipped off my sandal and kicked Skipper lightly. My bare foot prodded her knee under the table. Wendell Hawthorne III was wearing the kind of gaudy Rolex that could pay for a full semester of classes. I gave Skipper an encouraging look.

She sighed and looked up at him. "Why, that sounds nice, Wen. Do you have a business card?"

After he strutted off, his ego stroked and his dick half-hard, the three of us snickered and giggled. This was going to be easier than we'd imagined.

I leaned into the table and said in a low voice, "And that, my girls, is exactly how it's done. Skipper, you set up the date for Friday. Tomorrow night we'll meet to go through the process you'll use when you go back to his place for a nightcap. Mary-Ann, Ginger, and I will be nearby, on call at all times, ready to come in and help. You knock him out, and we'll take him for whatever we can get."

She shivered. "Fine, but I'm not fucking that guy. He's whiter and skinnier than a sun-bleached chicken bone. Ugh."

Mary-Ann frowned. "Really? I think he's kinda cute. Bet he has a big dick."

"What makes you say that?" I asked.

"His fingers are long. And so are his feet."

"You see those expensive Italian leather shoes?" I asked them. "That's what you should be looking at. Because Mr. The Third is just the kind of fish we're wanting to order off the menu."

Skipper sighed. "I don't care about his johnson. But his house better be loaded with lobster." As she examined the business card under the dim yellow light of the shaded lamp overhead, her face shifted into a half-smile. "Wendell Hawthorne appears to be a partner in a law firm. A litigator. My favorite kind of fool. His office is downtown, near Faneuil Hall." She looked at me. "This could prove to be a pretty big fish we got on the end of the hotline."

"Yeah, and we've got to start somewhere. Might as well start with Moby-Dick," I said.

"Call me Ishmael." Skipper dropped the card in her battered leather satchel. "I've got to hit the road. I need my beauty sleep."

I doubted that, but we all got up to leave. Tomorrow was another day, one in which we'd begin planning our first fuck 'n' grab.

On our way out the front door, Skipper made sure to catch the mark's eye. He was seated at the bar, alone, looking morose. But when he spotted her friendly wave, his face lit up. He grinned and waved back. The poor guy looked thrilled to death.

Chapter Four

I was three cups of Colombian dark roast into a full pot when somebody knocked on my front door. Had to be Buck. I hadn't buzzed anyone into the building. Yelling, "Hold on," I pulled a ratty BU sweatshirt over my fuchsia teddy. I had a bit of a Jerry hangover. That man could go for hours. Whew.

I opened the door a crack. Surprise, surprise—Ginger. Obviously, she'd spent the night with Buck. This annoyed me so I said, "Can't it wait until noon?"

"Shit, sorry. I'm just heading out for coffee and wondered if you want to join me."

I opened the door all the way, and she followed me inside. In the sun-bathed living room, her wild curls caught the morning light and turned her tangles a juicy strawberry color. I loved her hair. Shirley Temple had nothing on this chick.

"Buck's busy baking," she explained with a shrug of her narrow shoulders. "I'm off today, so I figured I'd hang out until tonight's powwow."

"You mean Mr. B," I reminded her. "Where do you work?"

"Beadles. You know, the bead store chain?"

She glanced around my little apartment, which I admit looked like a minimalist installment at the Museum of Fine Art. I wasn't into clutter. Or material goods. I always liked to feel as if I could run away at any moment and I wouldn't be leaving anything of value behind. Besides, it was Antoine's apartment originally. Two months after he failed to return from what he'd claimed was a business trip to Sydney, I pawned almost everything of value. Then I redesigned the apartment *à la chez* Shea.

Ginger withheld comment and said, "I work at the one in Nahant, walking distance from where I live. Only four days a week, though, and I'm not on today. So I don't want to take the train home, only to turn around and come back in again later. For our meeting tonight."

It was nine a.m., barely. She had all day. Was she planning on spending it here? I narrowed my eyes. Maybe I needed to get to know her a little better.

"Coffee? I have bagels, too. And cream cheese. From the Schmear." I led the way to my kitchenette.

"What's the Schmear?" She settled into the single wrought-iron chair at my tiny kitchen table. "It sounds Jewish."

Duh. Had she been living in a cereal box?

"Where're you from, Ginger?" I poured her a large ceramic mug of coffee. I hoped she liked it black. I didn't have any cream. No sugar either. The kind of luxuries I'd trained myself not to need anymore. Want, yes. Need, no.

"Nahant. Born and raised. Still live on the same street, six blocks from the ocean. But not with my parents. With my boyfriend. He's a sculptor. And a medical student. Former medical student." She shrugged, sipped her coffee. She didn't ask for milk and sugar. "He dropped out when he got commissioned by the Lexington Historical Society. He's creating a miniature replica of the Minuteman statue for some whatever-year centennial event. They're paying him big bucks."

I nodded, thinking about how he must have been the kind of boyfriend who didn't mind if his girlfriend stayed out all night.

I didn't say that, though. Instead, I got around to it. "Let me ask you something. You said in our interview that you need extra income. That you had experience in making money the dirty way. I'm taking you at your word. Plus, I like you." We smiled at one another. Her eyes were the green of sea glass. The kind of glass made smooth over time from the gentle rock of ocean waves against a shard from a Molson's bottle. "But this job is going to require nights spent away from your boyfriend. Nights on the prowl and on the run. How's this going to work for you two?"

"He's not that kind of boyfriend."

I split two pumpernickel bagels and set them on a flamingo pink ceramic dinner plate. I got out the generic brand cream cheese, a butter knife, and two dessert plates.

She sighed. "Hammond's the kind of boyfriend who sells his girlfriend for extra cash. If you know what I mean."

So that was the experience she'd mentioned. Sick fuck boyfriend experience. Many of us had it. I'd tangled with a handful of guys who wanted to see me bed their friends, or my friends, or both. Never for money, though. Actual sex for money transactions had come later. Like, the other day.

"How's that working out for you?" I set the plates

on the kitchen table, then leaned against the tile counter, dunking my bagel half in what was left of my coffee. "You making good money?"

She picked up her plate, held it steady, and put it down again. Suddenly, she dropped her face into her hands. Her shoulders shook as she sobbed silently. I swallowed a lump of barely chewed bagel. Shit. This girl was fragile. My interviewing skills had been worse than I thought. I blamed the chronic.

When Ginger looked up, her eyes were bright. Her voice hardened. "I hate it. He says it's *fun* and a *big turn on*, but it's all about funding his habit. And he doesn't respect me anymore. Maybe he never did."

Two fat tears ran down her prominent cheekbones and dripped off her pointy chin. None followed, and she wiped her face with the sleeve of her tangerine-colored cotton sweater. Which clashed fabulously with her hair. "I need to leave him. But I can't exactly move in with Buck. I mean Mr. B. He's just my supplier."

Aha. Now I got the blueprint. She came to see Buck, trading herself for weed discounts for her boyfriend. A friend with benefits, only the benefits went to her boyfriend. No wonder old Hammond didn't care if she stayed out all night.

I refilled her coffee cup and handed her a paper napkin. "Once we get things rolling, you'll be able to pay for your boyfriend's weed. Or move out. Whatever you choose. That's the whole point, becoming economically viable." I thought for a moment. "Look. If you want, you can stay here on the nights we work. I'm clean, I'm quiet, and I guarantee privacy. But no more fucking around with Mr. B. That could mess up our crew if you and him…"

I let the warning trail off, enough said.

She looked at me, smiled, and cocked her head. "He's a sweetheart. But he's in love with somebody else." She gave me an unfathomable look, then reached for the cream cheese. "I get what you're saying, and I appreciate the offer. So you really won't mind if I sleep on your couch?"

We both eyed the sleek magenta velveteen divan in the middle of the living room. I'd purchased it for next to nothing at the vintage store on Centre Street. I wouldn't have made a layover offer to just anyone, but Ginger was as thin as I was. She'd fit, but just barely, on the narrow couch. I did all right whenever I crashed there, like after watching romantic comedies on TV until I passed out, stupid and sated.

The apartment was really small, eight hundred square feet specially designed to meet the needs of a single tenant or a love-blinded couple. For two women, the tight conditions would be a strain. But we could give it a try. Maybe we could make it work temporarily. It would only be a few nights a week. Soon enough, Ginger would be better funded. Then she could stay overnight in her own city apartment.

"You can start off with this as home base on the nights we work," I told her. "Nahant is too far from the action. You'll need something in town. Eventually. So, until you get your own place, I think it's a good idea for you to stay here. No sense sitting on the train in the middle of the night, attracting attention."

I poured myself a little more coffee. I was wired. And pumped up, psyched for the crew to get started. "So, why don't you bring a suitcase next time you come into town? Looks like we may have our first gig on

Friday night."

In my mind, I was already clearing off a shelf for her in the bathroom medicine cabinet, a drawer in the breakfront across from the couch. It could work, as long as she wasn't a yakker. I'd go nuts if she turned out to be one of those women who feel the need to converse all day. And night!

Ginger jumped up and hugged me. Her hair actually smelled like ripe strawberries. It was uncanny.

"Thank you for being so nice to me," she mumbled. "I really, really need this. I need to change my life so bad. And you're making it happen. I owe you, big time."

I eased out of her damp clutch. Even though it was early in the day and early in the summer, it was already hot. My air-conditioning consisted of a floor fan in the bedroom. "Thank me after we knock off our first mark. Then we can see who owes who."

We finished our bagels and coffee in blessed silence. Then she told me she was going out for the afternoon and would see me later that night for the crew meeting.

She rinsed out her coffee cup and left my apartment. There was no trace of her except for the faint smell of fresh berries.

I liked her style. I really did.

****

Two more cups of Colombian later, I'd familiarized myself with the most widely available choices in modern knock-out drugs. I needed to learn how to make what they used to call a mickey. Short for Mickey Finn.

The infamous and potent drug-alcohol concoction

40

had been birthed in Chicago, named after the nineteenth century bartender who added chemical drops to the drinks he served so that he could rob his customers. Alcohol plus chloral hydrate equaled blackout, immobility, amnesia. And a huge "tip" for the devious bartender, who left his unconscious patrons in a back alley. When they awoke, the mild memory loss led them to believe they'd been rolled after leaving Finn's bar.

These days, all the underground knock-out drugs are referred to by other names. Liquid E. Special K. Roofies. Liquid X. Fantasy. After I crawled the Internet, I made a list of possibilities and went downstairs to see Buck. He'd supplied me with girls. Now he needed to supply me with knock-out drugs. Both were within his area of expertise, so I wasn't worried about him turning me down. But would our arrangement prove equitable? It all depended on the cut he'd lay claim to. We had yet to iron out that essential detail.

He answered on the first knock. No shirt, no shoes, no doubt in my mind he was the sexiest man in the building. In the neighborhood. Maybe for miles around. I sighed, followed his cute ass in gray sweats past the clutter and into the living area. Except for a corner where he'd camped out with his breakfast, the couch was piled with packaged product. There was nowhere to sit so I stood there, sharing what I was thinking.

"Like I told you, I don't want to be involved in something that illegal," he said between bites of what looked like eggs McMarijuana. "Consequences for someone like me could be a lifestyle crusher."

Peter Tosh did his thing on low volume from an

iPod in the kitchen area. I pointed to the mound of illegal drugs Buck sat next to and said, "Oh yeah, I get all that. But how many years you been doing this and how many years you want to *keep* doing this?" I paused while we locked stares. "I don't know about you, but I have serious life goals. Plans that cost money. And I've got debt I need to pay off. So I can have the life I want. Fucking college loans? *That's* the lifestyle crusher."

I held my breath. We were in one another's eyes now. Deep enough that I felt his heart race. Unless that was mine.

"Buck, listen to me. Just like you, I'm not into a life of crime. You know me, I'm not that sort of person either. But I plan to get past all that fast. Maybe in a few months' time. Then I'll go back to my normal life." Pointing to the kitchen stove, I added for emphasis, "You gonna bake ganja your whole life? Or what?"

He brushed muffin crumbs from his lips, sat back and stretched his arms along the back of the couch. His naked chest loomed like a warm bath after a cold night. How easy it would be to jump in his lap and cuddle there, let him hold me in his strong, hickory-smoked embrace. I turned away, walked slowly toward the door.

"This better not blow up in my face, Shea. But okay, I'll get you what you need."

I whipped around, shocked. I couldn't believe he'd changed his mind. And so quickly! "Heaven Scent," I said, automatically correcting him.

He gave me an odd look. "In addition to expenses, I'm gonna need ten percent of your take. Danger pay. I can get a lotta years for pushing benzodiazepines. Running narcotics is a whole echelon up the conviction ladder. Way different than selling medicinal brownies."

I nodded and Buck went back to his food.

The apartment smelled like sex, pot and toast. I watched Buck mop up egg yolk with an English muffin half. He hunched over his plate like he was still in the federal pen, protecting his food from the other offenders.

"Maybe this is all a bad idea," I said, suddenly scared. "Maybe the consequences are just too steep. For you, for me, for your girlfriends."

He looked up at me from his sliver of a seat on his cluttered madras sofa. I stared at the couch, which was loaded down with lunch bags full of special brownies, plus boxes of sandwich bags, baking sheets, tinfoil, and other tools of the trade. I knew that couch, I'd seen it at the vintage store. Underneath the mess he'd piled on the cushions, it looked functional. Like it would be a lot more comfortable than my divan. Why oh why did I always choose style over comfort?

"True, it's risky as hell," he said. "But the truth is, it's a brilliant idea. These guys, the marks, they're a bunch of putzes. Always on the hunt, looking for a night of free sex from beautiful young women who would never in a billion years sleep with them for real reasons. Not for lust, not for love. Women who will only fuck them for a material payoff. These guys are all a joke, they're just kidding themselves. So, we'll do them a favor. Give 'em a wake-up call."

He grinned. God, his teeth were white.

"Then they can turn around and file their overinflated insurance claims," he added.

Oh yeah, I reminded myself, trying to calm the questioning part of my brain, the smart area of the neocortex responsible for advancing civilization. Yes, this idea of mine was indeed brilliant. Because we'd get our money from people who had a lot more squirreled away. They'd all be the kind of one percenters with an endless supply wherever it was our score would be coming from. And these guys never lost. The marks would all file insurance claims, and get repaid. Likely they would claim even more than what we took from them. Oh yes, they'd be fine. They'd come out ahead, too. Everybody wins, right?

Buck sniffed. "All these upscale assholes, their insurance companies will cover their losses. Most they'll lose is a few hours of consciousness. Who knows, they may learn a little something. Maybe they won't think of women in the same stupid way anymore." He raised his bushy eyebrows, added, "Think of it like this, Shea."

I mouthed *Heaven Scent* at him, but he ignored me. He was too used to my given name. For that matter, had I called him Mr. B yet?

"Ultimately, we'll be ripping off the big insurance companies. The filthy rich corporations, the dirtiest of the dirty bastards. These are the same people who have ruined health care in this country. The ones who've wrecked small businesses, who make it impossible for a smart girl like you to get a decent job."

He thought I was smart? I smiled at Buck, straightened my shoulders. "Nice speech. Tell it to your parole officer."

"Oh, I have," he said. "Every time he points out how I had a scholarship to Berkeley. That's when I remind him the take on that gig didn't nearly cover the cost of living in a city like this."

He shook his head and the dreadlocks rustled around on his bare shoulders, his broad brown back. Today his hair looked like a stallion's mane, chestnut colored in the sunlight, and invitingly tangled. I wanted to brush through it with my hands, bury my face in it.

"I couldn't sell myself, not like you. I'm not pretty enough," he joked. I disagreed, but didn't say so. "So I had to design a business plan I knew would work for me. Sounds like you've done the same thing. I can understand that."

When he stood up, Buck towered over me, but in a nice way.

"You have a good head on your shoulders, Shea. I'm going to trust you. We can be smart about this, make it work for us. After all, times are tough. And only a few things are recession-proof. Sex is one, you got that covered. Booze intakes go up in a bad economy. As do the sales of drugs, which I'm on top of here, with my business. So we'll combine forces. We'll weather the rocky times with a bit of a merger."

He held out his hand and I took it. We shook, but he didn't let go. His palm was nice and smooth, warm. There was tension in the air, a crackling electric tension.

I pulled my hand away. "How soon can you get me some Liquid Ecstasy?" I asked my new business associate.

Liquid E, or Liquid X. Also known as GHB. Gamma-hydroxybutyric acid. From what I'd read, the drug was fast acting, and it was rarely detectable afterward in the blood or urine. Colorless, odorless, tasteless. Wouldn't kill anybody, but in the right dose it would send a big man to dreamland for several hours.

What's not to like?

Buck grinned. "I can have that to you in less than an hour. How's that for efficiency?"

I laughed. So what if I'd already rescinded sixty percent of the crew's take? With fifty going to Cedrick7Z and ten to Buck, us girls would have to split the remaining forty percent. Which meant that each of us would get ten percent, minus expenses. If we lifted as little as two or three Rolexes a week, I figured, we could be paying our bills. And then some.

It sure beat sucking dick. My new career barometer—was the job preferable to selling a blowjob to a creepy stranger? If yes, sign me up.

I said to Buck, "Please let me know as soon as you get the E. You can bring some to our crew meeting tonight. The girls will need to test it out, make sure it does what it's supposed to do." I moved toward the door.

"I ain't volunteering to be your first guinea pig," he said.

"Nobody's asking you to. But hey, you got any dumb friends who might not get what we're up to? Any exhausted friends who need a few extra hours of sleep tonight?"

Buck snorted. "I always have more than enough dumb friends. But you should experiment on someone we don't know. Safer that way. If nothing happens, we go back to the drawing board on drug selection. If he passes out, stays out, then you girls leave him be. Time the blackout. See what kind of noise disturbs him, if any. Test the whole setup, analyze it carefully."

He ran his eyes up and down my body. I shivered. I was still in my old alma mater sweatshirt and the lacy teddy. What was wrong with me, prancing around this man in my bedclothes?

"When your mark finally wakes up, your girl acts concerned," he continued. "She asks if he has a medical problem. Afterward, he thinks he just drank too much. Hopefully, he remembers very little about what actually happened. No questions, no problems? Then you're ready for a real shakedown."

I nodded. "Makes sense. Okay, get me the E and we'll do a dry run tonight. If all goes well, then we're good to go. Skipper already has a lead on a live one for Friday night."

Buck nodded. "Nice."

He followed me to the front door, stood close enough that I could smell his smoky-sweet breath. "I don't have feelings for her," he said suddenly. "We're just friends. We do business. I hope you know that."

I stiffened. He was talking about Ginger, his fuck buddy. I shrugged. "You can feel whatever you want. But starting today, there's no more sex between crew members. Let's keep this professional. Only way to succeed is to be smart. Like you said. Which means professional. Impersonal. And we need to be able to trust one another. Sex only gets in the way. Agreed?"

He agreed, but the look on his face was anything but agreeable. His eyes darted away, and his frown made me think I'd disappointed him. Well, so what if I had? I was running a business here, not a dating service.

I let myself out and hurried back upstairs to get ready for the meeting. I planned to do this right. Dress professionally, do a PowerPoint presentation, serve iced tea. This was my first crew meeting and I was pumped. I could use the skills I'd learned in school. Finally, I was going to be a teacher! Not the kind of professor I'd hoped to become, pacing a college classroom discussing *Beowulf*. But I'd be teaching just the same. Teaching women how to pay off debt and surmounting financial obstacles one drugged up mark at a time. As their handler, I'd show my crew how to spot a target, seduce him, knock him out, and take all his bling. Even though I'd never done anything remotely like that in my life.

Well, you know what they say? Those who can, do; those who can't, teach.

I sat down at my laptop and began working on my presentation. I was happy. My life was looking up.

Chapter Five

"I see a guy I wouldn't mind doing," Mary-Ann said in a loud voice. The other girls shushed her. "Well, I wouldn't. He's kinda cute."

We were in Señor Cancun's again, sitting in a booth. But we weren't drinking this time. I'd ordered a cup of coffee and loaded it up with all the cream and sugar I wanted. With any luck, we'd be up late tonight. The crew sipped ginger ales and diet colas, munched on the free chips and salsa Jerry had donated. No small talk, though. We were all business tonight, hot on the prowl for a subject to experiment on.

I looked around the crowded barroom. Tuesday was tequila night—buy one shot, get one free. The weekly event brought in a lot of partiers, so there was a wide selection available. But we needed just the right kind of guinea pig. We needed a guy who was wasn't too drunk. Alcohol and GHB don't go so well together. It's easy to overdo, make somebody sick. Or comatose. Our man needed to be relaxed, maybe a little bit high, but not bombed out. Just feeling good enough that one of us could convince him to come back to my place. Where we could drug him and observe the results.

In other words, we needed a willing victim. A nearly sober patsy who would unknowingly volunteer to serve as our first specimen.

"Which guy do you mean?" I asked Mary-Ann.

There wasn't a good-looking man within a hundred yards. Not as far as I could see. I scanned the dark room beneath the neon signs for Corona and Tecate, the string of little orange and red lights shaped like hot peppers, the booze-splattered mirror. The bar stools were loaded with drunks, mostly old guys in work pants drinking draft beer with their shots. Could these guys still get it up? Did they even care to?

I checked out the rest of the barroom. Tables of office workers huddled over piles of sucked limes, college kids hoisting shot glasses. The usual motley collection of loners slumped in their chairs, staring forlornly at the rapidly amassing line-up of empties. A half-dozen booths were filled with businessmen, faces red, neckties loosened. One booth featured an intertwined couple, their heads so close together you'd have to crowbar them apart.

The Grand Magnolias rocked on grandly over the restaurant's meh sound system. I shook my head. Not a potential mark in sight. The bar tonight did not seem promising. Why would it? Our plan was to frequent uptown nightclubs with upscale patrons. Not low rent hangouts down the street from my apartment.

We were staying close to home tonight, however, to limit the unknowns during our first attempt. A controlled practice run. Only once we were confident in our ability to handle a mark would we race with the alpha dogs.

"Here he comes," Mary-Ann whispered. "He was in the restroom. Oh, Jaysus. He's so cute."

I followed her gaze to the back of the bar where the men's room was located. Yup. He was a looker all right. Tall, well-built, dark brown hair in a thick wavy mop. Nice tight jeans. Plus, he was alone, and he was ready for us. The way he dropped into his seat at a table in the back, he'd had a few already. But he wasn't falling-down drunk, just defeated. Heavy hearted. In a low mood and ripe for a conning.

Mary-Ann and I watched carefully as the mark sighed heavily, fiddled with the label on a bottle of Tecate. When he whipped out his phone and set it on the table, I knew for sure he was ours. Broad shoulders in a telltale slouch, our boy stared at his smart phone as if he were waiting for somebody, anybody, to call.

He was perfect.

I nodded at Mary-Ann, then leaned in to talk to my crew. "Okay, Mary-Ann is gonna take this one in," I told the others. "Let's get into position, girls."

We'd gone over everything in our meeting before walking to the bar. We all knew what to do. It wasn't brain surgery, just guy pickup 101.

Mary-Ann stood up. She smoothed down the wrinkles in her silky little dress, primping a bit as she flashed us a grin. Her ass did look adorable, and I told her that.

She laughed. "Hopefully, that will be all it takes. Either way, see you back at the joint. Give me thirty minutes."

"The joint" was my place. Slang for where a con takes down the mark, and for tonight's schedule of events, that would be my apartment. Conveniently located, and stocked up with Buck's afternoon score of Liquid E.

We watched Mary-Ann approach the mark, who had stripped the entire label from his beer bottle and switched to playing with his phone. His smiled up at her, a poor fish rescued from a sea of loneliness. Soon enough, he'd be hot on the grill.

I gave the girls the hand signal and we trooped out of the bar. A few dudes tried to talk to Skipper on the way out, but she just smiled vaguely and walked on past.

****

Less than an hour later, we were all in my living room. REM was blasting from the CD player, a half-dozen almond-scented candles blazed, and a man lay on his back on my couch. A man with his mouth open wide. A good looking, unconscious man.

I leaned over him and listened to his breathing. It was deep, sonorous. Gently, I unlaced his black Nikes and slid them off. Not a good idea to dirty up the divan. Ginger would be sleeping there soon enough.

"Poor Kyle. If we hadn't given him the E, I do believe he would have asked to walk me home. Carry my books. He was that into me."

Mary-Ann sprawled on the floor next to the couch in her bra and panties. Flimsy, lacy little items from the Victoria's Secret department at K-Mart. She ran a hand through Kyle's hair. "Seems like a nice enough guy." Her voice was wistful.

"How do you judge your men, Mary-Ann? By how cute they are? Or are there other qualities, actual useful credentials, you keep in mind when mating?" Skipper's voice was not as neutral, as nonjudgmental, as a therapist's should be. In fact, she seemed pissed off, standing by the kitchen counter, her back straight and tense.

"Are you asking about the fathers of my boys? Is

that your shit, girl?" Mary-Ann stood up, reaching for her mini-dress. It lay in a heap on the living room floor. Not a big heap, though. In fact, the dress pile, shimmery and silver, was around the size of a hand towel.

"My *shit* is to wonder if you're gonna fall in love with every man we rip off," Skipper said in a low, barely controlled voice. "My *shit* is to not end up with a criminal record that ruins my counseling career before I even get a chance to launch it."

"He's jiggling one of his feet," Ginger interrupted. "Think he can hear us?"

She had a ballpoint pen in one hand, a lined notepad in the other. I'd asked her to jot down times. How long it took Mary-Ann to lure him out of the bar—twenty minutes. How long it took him to take off Mary-Ann's dress after they'd settled onto the couch— one minute, maybe less. How long it took him to pass out after she handed him the doctored beer—twenty minutes, which was apparently enough time for Mary-Ann to fall for the guy. How much of the drugged drink he'd consumed before nodding off in her arms—less than half.

"He was jiggling something else a few minutes ago," Mary-Ann said with a saucy smile. "I was starting to get excited."

We all laughed. I bent closer to Kyle's prostrate form, an ear cocked to his deep breathing. He wasn't about to wake up. In fact, he seemed nearly comatose.

"Kyle?" I asked. "Can you hear me?"

No response. I lifted his right arm from his chest, let it drop. Plunk. He was lights out, all right.

"Okay, keep an eye on the clock," I said to Ginger and she nodded. "If he's out for two hours or longer, we'll know it works well enough to knock out and call in the troops to help rip off, then escape clean with the goods. We'll use around the same quantity of Liquid E every time. No more. We don't want to hurt anyone, right?"

Skipper said, "Should I start?" When I said sure, she told the others, "As if we're in the real joint, I'm picking up the take. And packing it up. Bling to go. Like I'd do with the mark's valuables. Ginger, can you time me?"

Ginger said, "Go."

While the two of them played out the rest of the heist, Mary-Ann sat on the edge of the couch, watching the mark. The specimen. The most recent man to undress her hot little bod. The sappy lovesick look on her face was freaking me out. We'd spied on her seduction from a crack in my bedroom door, and Kyle seemed to be the one who was into it. He was all over Mary-Ann. Not the other way around.

Now she was the one who looked lovelorn. Her eyes were glazed, haunted. Like she wanted to devour the guy, drag him back to her woman-cave in Dorchester.

When he stuttered and let out a deep snore, Mary-Ann moved closer and stroked his forehead lightly. Tenderly.

Oh no.

"What, you have reverse Stockholm syndrome?" I asked her. "You fall in love with your captives?"

She kept her eyes on Kyle's sleeping face. "He works at the liquor store on Centre Street. He told me he makes deliveries to the old people who can't go pick up their booze anymore." She sighed. "He shouldn't drink. Ruins his judgment. If he didn't drink, he might make somebody a nice partner."

"Maybe after tonight he'll quit. If I passed out in a stranger's apartment, I know I'd go off the sauce. Maybe we will be just the impetus he needs to decide to go straight."

I didn't believe it myself, but it sounded plausible. Like what Buck had been saying about us doing right while we were doing wrong. Hey, who said we couldn't be mythic grifters, whores with the proverbial hearts of gold? The kind of trickster seductresses who lead you astray to teach you a lesson, make you a better person. Everybody wins, right?

"Just don't start thinking you want to see this guy again, Mary-Ann," I warned. Her small fingers were toying with Kyle's moist lips. "After tonight, he's off-limits. He could get suspicious, turn on you. We can't take the risk. Okay?"

She nodded ever so slightly. It was not reassuring.

Skipper double slapped the front door and announced, "Done." On her shoulder, one of the collapsible plastic backpacks I'd purchased for us to use for hauling stash. Her black sack was stuffed with whatever she'd rustled up around my apartment. "Time?"

"Seven and a half minutes," Ginger said. "What did you grab?"

"Heaven here has some badass jewelry," Skipper laughed. "If I could, I'd keep most of it. I like the turquoise. Nice stuff, girlfriend. I'd also keep this little ashtray with the pretty shells all over it. Love it."

She rummaged through the pack, held up the knickknack.

Mickey J. Corrigan

Antoine had given me that pearly shell. He'd found it at some dive shop the first time we went to see my mom in St. Augustine. Back when he liked me. Back when *I* liked me.

"No can do," I said lightly.

Skipper gave me an *only kidding* wave. She began returning my goodies to their proper spots on bookshelves, in kitchen cabinets, and in my bedroom where I kept my ivory inlay jewelry box.

But my heart had dropped with a quiet splash and, after that, I wasn't as excited about how clever we'd been in seducing our first mark. Antoine had loved me, or so I had thought. But he'd left me holding the bag— debt, car, apartment, life. All without him. Being reminded of that bummed me out. How could he just take off like that without me? What was wrong with me? Was I that despicable?

At the start, we were totally in lust, together as often as possible between his gig as an investigative reporter for the startup website Tell All, and mine as a full-time grad student with a full-time tutoring job. We were both busy, always on the run, but we made time for one another. Yeah, we had our differences, and we bickered. In fact, we fought like animals, and we fought a lot. But the sex was awesome, so I practically lived at his place. And now that he was gone for good, I did live at his place. And occasionally—well, maybe more than occasionally—I was reminded of what had gone missing from my life.

Sanity. A man I could trust. Love. Sex with someone I cared about. A shot at a decent future. Self-respect.

"How long has he been out?" Skipper asked

56

Ginger. She was on her second cup of coffee from the pot I'd brewed for Kyle to drink later, when he came to. Now she was pacing up and down the hallway. With her long legs, she could go from the front door to the kitchenette in seven or eight strides. Watching her was dizzying. "I'm not good at sitting around, waiting for men to wake up. I always make them leave *before* they fall asleep."

"Right on, sistah," Mary-Ann said. This, however, I didn't buy her feminist act. Neither did Skipper, who shook her head and kept pacing.

"Thirty-nine minutes," Ginger reported, looking up from her digital watch. "We have at least another hour to wait. So maybe you can sit down and relax or something. You're starting to make me nervous."

Skipper could be sort of hyper, and she was antsy when you penned her in. She'd been like a big horse in a small barn while we waited in my bedroom for the drug to take effect on Kyle. Now I was wondering how calm she would be in the trenches.

She knew what I was thinking and said, "I'm usually chiller than this. Sorry. Must've had too much caffeine. I'll take a chill pill." She sat down at the kitchen table, crossed her super long legs, which looked even longer in a pair of black running tights, and gave me an anxious smile.

Hanging around, the five of us squeezed together in my hot little apartment, wasn't helping any of us to stay chill. As I snuffed the candles and turned down the music, I apologized for the tight quarters. "Remember, next time it will be you and a man in a hotel room or a waterfront condo or a Spanish-Mediterranean out in the 'burbs. Your next gig will be a lot less claustrophobic.

Or should be."

Skipper nodded. "Wen's meeting me at the wharf at seven-thirty on Friday. I think I'm ready. But I don't know. I'm kind of freaked about it. About him."

Mary-Ann finally left the sleeping guinea pig and wandered toward the kitchen. "You'll do great, Skip. He'll be mush in your hands. If I can score in, what was it, forty-one minutes? You'll be in and out in half the time."

"Maybe," Skipper said, a bemused look on her face. "But you were into this Kyle guy. I'm not gonna be with my mark. I'll have to put on a terrific act. Because that man, Wendell Hawthorn the Third? He gives me the heebie-jeebies." She wrinkled up her nose, then shrugged. "Not saying I can't do it, just that it won't be a turn on. At least, not for me."

We tried to reassure her, but ultimately, she'd have to face her demons alone. Like we all do.

When Kyle woke up two hours later, he groaned and held his head in his hands. After he apologized for falling asleep and admitted he felt too woozy to drive, Skipper volunteered to take him home. Mary-Ann seemed a little too happy to tag along.

Ginger and I crashed out, both of us tumbling into sleep as if we were the ones who'd been drugged. I had weird, frightening, nightmarish dreams. Each time, I woke myself up, my entire body shaking all over. I didn't know what was scaring me, though. The dreams were eerie, fleeting and dim. Like shadows drifting over my bed.

Around five a.m., I got up and wandered out to the living room. The gauzy yellow street light fell softly on the wood floor, trailing across my couch and up the front of Antoine's ludicrously expensive entertainment center. That was one item I had yet to pawn. Men sure knew how to buy the best technology.

I sighed. Over on the divan, Ginger looked peaceful. Her amazing hair fluffed around her head, clashing sharply with the maroon plush of the couch. She looked like Lucille Ball as rendered by Picasso. If I'd had any artistic talent, I would have wanted to paint the scene.

Giving up on sleep for the night, I padded out to the kitchen and brewed up more Colombian until it smelled like morning. Another day, another day closer to financial success. I sat at the table and drank black coffee until my crewmate woke up.

Chapter Six

On Friday morning, I had a tutoring session with Freeman Dorff, a smart but lazy sophomore whose family was willing to pay me a few bucks in the hope he could eventually ace his SATs. Like I had when I was his age.

We met up in front of the Boston Public Library at ten. When he spotted me running up the wide marble steps, Freeman slowly removed his ear buds. He flashed a post-ironic grin, his braces bright in the morning sunlight.

"Hey, Prof."

"Hey yourself," I said.

He tucked his pockmarked skateboard under one skinny arm, then led the way inside the massive building. We walked in a circle, looking for an empty table where we could spread out and talk without bothering anyone. As we passed a kid in a white hoodie loitering by the stacks, Freeman gave him the too-cool-to-talk hi sign. Then he commandeered a couple chairs in a corner, and we got to work on grammar and punctuation.

An hour and a half later, my sole summer student was tired of rewriting short dumb essays and I was getting a boredom headache. When I agreed we were done for the day, he gave me the peace-out sign and packed up his tablet. Before he cantered away, though, he searched the pockets of his cargo shorts, then handed me a check. A hundred bucks, and my mouth didn't even hurt. Too bad I didn't have twenty more students like Freeman.

His mother had hired me a few years before to tutor her oldest boy, now a junior at Yale. She was hoping for similar stellar results with the younger one. My call—major longshot. Motivated kids get into the ivy league schools. Skateboarders go to community college.

Even though I didn't do much tutoring anymore now that I was no longer affiliated with any of the local institutes of higher education, Mrs. Dorff still wanted me for the job. I liked the woman. A no nonsense type who dressed in starched cotton and sensible pumps, she lived in a beautiful penthouse condo overlooking the Charles River. Once in a while, I got to enjoy the view when she invited me to lunch. We talked books. Mrs. Dorff was a big reader. Mr. Dorff traveled a lot on business. I'd never met him. She seemed a bit like a kept woman, but one with great style and a heavy dose of New England reserve.

With a little mad money burning a hole in my jean skirt pocket, I strolled down Comm. Ave., enjoying the fresh spring air. The buildings sparkled in the noontime sun. Robins called to one another as they flew by, pigeons cooed from their messy nests on narrow window ledges. If you didn't notice all the trash blowing around the filthy sidewalks, the city could look pretty nice sometimes.

When I got to Symphony Hall, I abandoned my walk and jumped on the T. The car was nearly empty, just a young guy in a blazing white hoodie and me. I sat in one of the molded plastic seats and watched out the window as we trundled past Northeastern.

One day, I'll be taking classes there again. One day, I'll be teaching there. One day.

Shea's pathetic little mantra.

I got off the train at the top of the hill and walked the few blocks to my apartment building. The air had thickened somewhat, threatening to heat up to an uncomfortable degree, but there was a delicious breeze off the pond. I sniffed. Sure enough, the soft scent of lilacs rode on the light wind. Another delightful springtime treat in a city not well-known for its flora.

Just as I turned up the front walkway to my building, a ponytailed mail person in blue uniform shorts pushed out the front door. She stopped when she saw me and reached into the big brown bag she'd hooked over one shoulder. When I met up with her on the steps, she handed me a thick packet of business envelopes, magazines and fliers. "You got to empty out your mailbox, sweetheart. I can't fit nothing else in there."

I thanked her and went into the lobby to deal with my mail. I planned to clean out the box, clear out everything I'd ignored over the past few weeks. I hated collecting my mail, mainly because I was afraid to face the truth. My debts were closing in on me. Fast.

The little glass mailbox was stuffed to the gills with bills, ads, and other unwanted stuff sent to either me or Antoine. I sorted the crap from the chaff, dumping the junk in the garbage can by the front door, saving the past dues. An official looking envelope addressed to my missing boyfriend caught my eye. I tore it open. It was a warning from some collection agency for a financial institution. Antoine's college loans had gone unpaid for so long his total debt load was up to six figures.

I whistled, tucking the paperwork under one arm. I hadn't realized how bad his situation was. No wonder he'd fled to Australia. He would never be able to repay the loan now, not on his income from the fledgling website. TellAll.com had amassed a good-sized cult following, but their ad revenue was meager at best. At least, that had been the situation when Antoine and I were together. I wasn't even sure he was working for the site anymore. I certainly wasn't keeping up with whatever was going on in the blogosphere.

After a quick lunch consisting of sliced brown tomato and browning avocado on a piece of forgotten, week old, thick crust pizza, I did some research on my computer. Then I headed back downtown. I took the train again, then walked. The sky was cloudless, a searing blue. By the time I got to Beacon Street, I was sweating.

The crew was already at the café waiting for me. They were sitting at a sidewalk table drinking iced chai. I collapsed into a plastic chair. "Jeezus. Anybody ever hear of going inside where it's air conditioned?" I fanned myself with somebody's wrinkled copy of *Boston Magazine*, but it didn't help.

That's when I saw him again. The kid in the brighty-whitey sweatshirt. Same skinny body, same teenage slouch. Scuffed high-tops, scrunched brown face tucked inside the loose hood. He sauntered along the opposite side of Beacon, staring in shop windows.

"Weird." If it were coincidental, that would be

weird enough. But if the boy was actually following me? That would be creepy weird. "I've seen that guy three different times today."

"What guy?" Skipper craned her neck to see where I was staring. "Little gangbanger over there? Huh. How you even notice that pipsqueak, anyway?"

Mary-Ann laughed. "Should we grab the kid? Drug him up, find out what he's up to?" She looked oddly happy. I began to suspect her perky, upbeat mood had something to do with Kyle. "Want me to go over there, invite him to our table?"

Ginger and Skipper both said no, and I held up a hand. "Forget it. We have to focus on our plans for tonight. What've we decided? Do we hang out at a bar on the wharf near the restaurant to wait for Skipper or sit it out back at my place? Skipper? Thoughts?"

She shrugged. Her hair hung down her long back in a thick rope of a braid. Her face lean and clean, without a drop of makeup, she looked magnificent. Her muscular but sleek stance radiated sexual strength and power.

"I texted with him today on the disposable phone. I found out a few useful details." She shook her head, sighed.

I could tell the girl was getting nervous. Who wouldn't, with the clock ticking down to performance time?

"He's working on some high profile case, so he's at the office for twelve or fourteen hour days. He says he can spare a few hours, so that's a good sign. He lives in Malden. But I'm pretty sure he has a wife and family stashed there. Malden is a wife and family kind of place." She fiddled with her Styrofoam cup. "That would leave a local hotel. And if I can only grab what he has on him, well, that will really limit the take. To the Rolex, maybe some cash…"

"If he isn't wearing the watch or one a lot like it, excuse yourself after the meal and grab a cab. Then call us and we'll pick you up," I advised. "No sense wasting all night on a low pull."

She brightened at that, which worried me. Did she want out? Already?

"Maybe you guys can hang outside the restaurant, then follow me to the hotel and wait outside. Just in case I need some assistance."

Mary-Ann gave me a look. *WTF?*

"Look. This is your party, you run the show, Skip," I told her. "Men, they're bowled over by you. Smitten on first sight. You dictate what happens tonight. You tell old Wendell where you want to go after dinner. He'll take you there. If he wants to fuck you, which he will, of course. He already does. The man will do whatever you tell him to. Guaranteed."

She swallowed hard. "Maybe. But I'm used to pushing them off. Not inviting them into my vagina." She gave me an odd look, a mix between a pitiful plea and a guilty shrug. "He better not get any closer than a hand on my butt, or I might end up slapping his face. And that would wreck everything."

Sure would. I was about to warn her not to turn the man off before the E took effect, lest he kick her out and ruin our heist plans entirely. But Ginger cut me off.

"Let me tell you a little secret about making it with a man you find utterly distasteful." She tilted her head. Her hair was a golden red in the sunlight, her skin milky white. We all sat there, waiting for her to share her hard-earned wisdom. "You gotta close your eyes. Use your imagination. Pretend his hands are actually the hands of George Clooney. Or Brad Pitt, Ryan Gosling. Imagine you are the tantalizing lover of a gorgeous star, his beloved, and he has been away on location for so long you barely recognize his touch. Let yourself respond to that fantasy. And don't, whatever you do, open your eyes." She shrugged her freckled shoulders. "Basic acting techniques."

"You sound like you've done this yourself more than once. Boyfriend problems?" Skipper snapped. But when she saw Ginger's face crumple, she reached out to grab the other woman's hand. "Sorry, sorry. I'm being such a bitch. It's just that, I, well…" Her eyes darted around the table and back to Ginger. "Truth is, I'm frigid. So he better pass out quick or I'm going to be in big fucking trouble."

What?

"What does that even mean?" Mary-Ann asked, unfazed, a smile lingering on her pretty pink lips. "You like women?"

Skipper shook her head. "No, and I don't want to sleep with you, Mary-Ann. I'm not gay. I'm just not into sex. And this guy, he's icky." She sucked in her breath and blew it out. Her dark eyes were sad, apologetic. "I thought the seduction part of the gig would be a piece of cake. Then I watched you with Kyle the other night and, oh, shit. Truth hit me hard. For me, the time between drugging 'em and them passing out is gonna present a challenge."

Buck's muthafucking chronic! That pot had really messed with my head. Being baked on the night of the audition had made me see things that were simply not

66

there. Now my blinders were off, and it was clear as the afternoon sky. Mary-Ann was on the crew to snare a boyfriend. Ginger was hiding from an abusive lover. And Skipper wanted to drug-rob guys as revenge because she hated sex. Some girl gang. Why oh why had I eaten that mindblow of a brownie?

"It doesn't matter how you feel," Ginger said, "as long as he thinks you're into him. You're a terrific actor, Skipper. Nobody would ever guess you weren't as sexed up as you look."

Thank you, Ginger.

Skipper's glow of a smile lightened her face, and this immediately brightened the mood. "You really think I can pull it off?"

We patted her back and enthused wildly. But when she left to find the ladies room, the three of us fell silent.

"Fucking A," Mary-Ann finally said. "Tonight's gonna be a real nail biter. Wish we could be flies on the wall for this one."

Suddenly, I had a brilliant idea. "Hey, where's the nearest spyware store? Anybody know?"

Ginger was right with me. "Right. Good thinking. We wire her up, keep watch. Then we know instantly what we need to do to keep her going."

"GPS," I said. "A tiny tape recorder, maybe. A wearable camera. You can get glasses with hands-free video and audio functions."

"Is that even legal?" Mary-Ann asked.

I laughed. "As if that's something *we'd* be concerned about."

"Oh, right." Mary-Ann chewed on the end of her straw, then added, "But who has the money for high-tech equipment? Unless somebody has a credit card that's not overextended?"

The three of us looked at one another, shook our heads knowingly, and returned to our brooding. Fuck me, my confidence in the night ahead of us was really taking a nosedive. I needed to come up with a better plan than the one we'd agreed on earlier. Something tighter, and more comfortable for Skipper. Frigid? Who would ever have guessed that the sexiest woman in Boston hated sex?

When Skipper came back from the restroom, I stood up to face her. "Okay, here's what we'll do. We're going to park outside the restaurant. The whole time you're in there, we'll be out in the car. You pocket dial me when you can, leave your phone on. I'll put you on speaker. So the three of us can hear what's going on with you and the mark." Skipper was grinning now. "We'll be a few steps ahead of you this way. Ready to move to the joint before you get there. Ready to come help you if you need it. Ready at a moment's notice. No worries."

She grabbed me by the waist and gave me a huge squeeze. Man, she was strong. She really didn't have to worry about The Third. She could probably wrestle the guy to the ground even without drugging him. Even with one arm tied behind her back. Hopefully, though, the mark wouldn't be into bondage. I chuckled to myself. For his sake, Wendell Hawthorne III better not talk BSDM. She might kick his ass for even suggesting it.

"Thanks, Heaven. All of you, thanks. Sorry I'm being such a pussy."

We reassured her, said all the right things. Like

nonsense, don't worry about it. But Skipper was right. She *was* being a pussy. And con games are not for pussies.

I had to go back to JP to pick up the Mini. So we arranged to meet a block west of the wharf at seven p.m. Skipper, of course, would arrive fashionably late. And she would be on her own. We all gave her a few more verbal high-fives before we split up.

I walked toward the train station on Park. The streets were crowded, loud and thick with horn-blowing, slow-moving, Friday afternoon traffic. It was going to be a bitch to find a parking space near the restaurant later. But we couldn't use the valet service, of course, or the private parking lot. Because we were not going to be patrons. The same situation would apply when the happy couple moved on to the joint. Especially if it turned out to be a downtown hotel. I'd have to park the car on the street then, too. Shit.

I mulled over the situation while waiting for the green line. Standing there at the Park Street station in the midst of a boisterous post-work throng, I thought I saw a flash of white hoodie. But when I turned around, it was gone.

Chapter Seven

I met Antoine when I was twenty-one, a college student, and relatively new to Señor Cancun's. This was before the dive was my hangout, before Jamaica Plain was my town. Jerry was working the bar that night. We were already casual lovers, buddy lovers, so I was sitting on a stool talking to him and some of the regulars. It was a Tuesday. We were all doing shots of tequila.

Then this man, this beautiful man, sat down on the stool right beside me. Antoine.

Tall, thin, pale as ice. Eyes like a winter sky. His stark beauty, his glacial features, were so unusual they freaked me out. Holy shit, the guy was awesome.

I didn't speak to him at first, but I sure noticed him. The man had presence. It was like sitting next to an Alaskan Husky but without the panting or the drool.

"So this guy comes in again and I tell him, 'Buddy, you're shut off, man. I don't wanna get sued when you floor your car in reverse and mow down a buncha pedestrians.' And the guy takes out a hundred dollar bill, says, 'This change your mind, big fella?' S'when the second guy comes in, he looks like a brother from Southie, I hadda just shut my mouth, take the…"

I was having trouble focusing on what Jerry was yakking about. Antoine's physical proximity was that distracting. Enough that I slid my bar stool farther away. Still, there he was, seeping into my consciousness like a forgotten dream.

Jerry kept on with his tall bartender tale. Trying not to look, I sensed my seatmate was listening to Jerry, too, while sipping on his draft beer. Every now and then, I would feel his eyes on me. Roving across my face, my bust, the rest of my body. Appraising me. Sizing me up. I didn't stare back at him, but I wanted to. I didn't invite him into the conversation, but I wanted to do that, too. Instead, I stayed chill. I let him come to me. Which, eventually, he did.

But first, he sent Jerry to fetch a second draft. Once my bartender's broad back was turned, Antoine leaned over to whisper in my ear.

The first words he said to me? "You look like a mermaid."

I sat back. Huh? I stared into his ice pop eyes while he continued.

"You know that famous John William Waterhouse painting of a mermaid? Anyone ever tell you how much you look like her?" His voice was sexy, low. He smelled minty, and musky.

I shook my head. I wasn't much of an art aficionado.

"Ever see the bow of an old ship? The carved figureheads of mermaids who kept the ship safe from sea monsters, pirates, other harmful threats? That's who you remind me of." He had the nicest chin with a sweet little cleft in it.

I didn't know how to react. Since it was tequila night, I'd downed a couple shots already, so instead of being sophisticated about it, I blushed hard. Then I laughed at him, but really, I was embarrassed as all hell.

The flushing heated my face so much that I finally had to shrug him off, turn away.

In the end, I said nothing in response. Frazzled, I chose to ignore him. Later, when I thought about what the cool man with the long black hair, the fine angular face, the albino skin and pale blue eyes had said to me, it brought a smile to my face. Still does. Me, a mermaid? I don't even swim.

Jerry came back, noticed nothing, and started yakking again. "The Southie guy, turns out, is the grand-nephew of the guy Whitey hired to…"

I half-listened to another one of Jerry's mobster tales, nodding in all the right places. Whenever I glanced at Antoine, he was staring at me. He'd simply smile, flashing teeth white as an iceberg. I had to smile back. The guy was that mesmerizing.

Still, we didn't talk much that night because it would have pissed off Jerry. Not that he was my boyfriend, just that men in general can be weirdly possessive. Antoine was intelligent enough to understand this little game and interested enough in me that he was willing to play along.

Jerry liked showing off for me. That's how we met in the first place. I wandered in for a cold beer; he showed off. Then we fucked. That was about it. Jerry was the kind of guy who worked at being the focus of attention while he juggled six drinks at once or tossed an obnoxious drunk out the front door by the seat of his pants. Big, cute, entertaining, Jerry had lots of customers and an odd lot of friends. Politicians and gangsters, punks and bankers, bikers and writers. Because of his gregarious nature, he had lots of stories to tell. Jerry was amusing.

But Antoine? Antoine was intoxicating.

The attractive stranger left before I did that night because I was there for the long haul, waiting until Jerry got off work. After he'd finished his third and final light beer, the intriguing man with the unusual pickup lines stood and stretched his long limbs. My heart crawled up my throat and grabbed onto my tongue. Wow, he was tall. Had to be six-foot four. When he held out a hand, I took it. Clean hands, no callouses. I could smell wintergreen.

He leaned down, way down, and whispered in my ear, "Hope we meet again, mermaid."

I couldn't help it, I grinned. But my body betrayed me and I started blushing again. I was heating up uncontrollably, so on fire I had to fan my face with my palms. He took advantage of my discomfort to slip me his business card.

"Call me, if you want to get coffee some afternoon."

Such a gentleman. Watching him stroll out of the bar, I put one hand to my chest. Heart, be still. The man was so cool he was the ultimate chill. And he walked like he knew where he was going. What a turn on. I tucked the embossed card into the front pocket of my jeans, where it seared the delicate crease in my thigh.

An hour later, I was riding Jerry and not thinking about Antoine. Much.

The next night, I was home, crashing at my house share in the suburbs. Four of my six roommates were drinking beers and grilling out on the back porch. I lay on my funky futon, sniffing sweet lamb with cherry tomatoes and staring at the card Antoine had given me. Apparently, Mr. Antoine Locke worked as a journalist for *Spyguy Magazine*, in their Boston office. I moved over to my laptop and, before I could talk myself out of it, dashed off a lighthearted and flirtatious email.

He responded instantly, asking for my phone number, which I quickly sent to him. Then I headed downstairs to see whether my roommates had any leftover kebobs. The evening was cool, with a scent of autumn in the air.

Just as I stepped outside, my phone rang. Antoine.

"Hi," he said. "You want to get that coffee?"

The man got right to the point. Made me wonder what sex would be like. Fast and direct, I assumed. My heart rushed around in my chest like a nervous waitress.

"I *am* a caffeine addict," I admitted. "Should we meet one day this week?"

"How about in half an hour. In Harvard Square? Halfway between us."

How did he know where I lived?

He read my mind, then eased it. "Your telephone exchange is Newton. Unless you bought the phone there and live elsewhere?"

Spyguy had me there. I was wowed by his take-command style. He knew what he wanted and he went for it. What woman doesn't admire that in a man?

"I can meet you in Cambridge, sure. Which café you thinking about?"

He told me. We hung up, and I ran right back upstairs to change. Low-cut silk blouse, denim skirt, short black boots. I had to wait for the T, but I was traveling against the commuter traffic so I made it to Cambridge in forty minutes. The Au Bon Pain was packed, as always, but my date had scored us one of the wrought-iron tables out front.

He stood up when I approached. Such a gentleman. Dressed in an expensive gray suit and a lovely green silk tie, he looked even more stunning than he had at Cancun's. I must have been ogling him in his business attire because he pointed to his jacket lapel. "Had an important meeting with the publisher today. Trying to look sharp so they don't have an excuse to fire me."

"Are they looking for one?"

He nodded. "With me, they usually are." He stared at me for a minute, smiling his dazzling smile. "My interviewing techniques are controversial."

"You waterboarding your sources?"

He laughed. "Something like that. Can I buy you a coffee?"

I said sure and sat down. My date went inside and fetched us espressos, biscotti, and a couple of delicious blueberry scones. I could get fat with this man. An appealing idea.

We talked about ourselves, our histories, our plans for our futures. We talked until the streets had emptied out. Then he walked me to the T stop. We got on different trains, me back to the 'burbs and Antoine into town to return to his office. Where he worked all night. I know because he sent me an email at four a.m. telling me he enjoyed talking to me and when he finished the piece he was writing, crashed and recovered, we might want to grab lunch.

So, coffee in Harvard Square led to lunch a few days later on Newberry Street. Dinner the following Saturday night and a romcom movie in chichi Lexington led to a string of other dates. I liked him. I lusted after him. He courted me. Until finally, all the talking and eye contact and light accidental touching and hand holding and kisses goodbye, lingering kisses goodbye, led to us getting naked together and giving it our all. This worked just fine, better than fine, and led to us spending our free time in his apartment in Jamaica Plain, having a lot of great sex and way too many arguments.

Antoine said he was crazy about me, but his rules were restrictive and chafing. He was gone all the time, working round the clock. Yet he was controlling about my comings and goings. I was busy with school and work, but I did have an active social life. And, I will admit, I was not very good at the monogamy thing.

This was prior to my hooking career, of course, because I met Antoine back when I was still an undergraduate, still all dreamy eyed about my career in education. So I was clean, totally legal, and my libido was operating overtime. Antoine appreciated this about me, but he was insistent that nobody else should be able to share his enthusiasm.

In order to maintain calm in the relationship, my in-and-outings with Jerry had to go. The rest of my one-hour boyfriends had to go, too. I didn't like it, but I complied to keep the fragile peace between us. However, when Antoine left his job at *Spyguy* to work as an investigative reporter for the Tell All startup, he began logging even longer hours than before. So, in my final year at BU, suffering a bad case of senioritis, I grew resentful. I felt trapped. With Antoine gone all the time, I became bored, antsy for more zing in my life.

Buck befriended me one spring night when I was hanging out on the front steps, drinking a glass of screw-top red. We clicked right off. He was easy to talk to, plus he had weed galore. I needed a friend to while away the time I spent waiting for Antoine to come home.

I started dropping by Buck's studio whenever I had nothing going on upstairs. Which occurred all too often. We sat around his place, chatting and getting high. This annoyed Antoine, who encouraged me to apply to a graduate program so I could move up the career ladder from college-prep tutoring to full-time college teaching. He was right. That was the dream. Only a part of me wasn't ready for the commitment. And the rest of me didn't understand the loan ramifications.

While I applied to several local universities, Antoine worked seventy-hour weeks. Every other month, he traveled. Sometimes he was gone for a week or more. I had too much time on my hands not to get into trouble. But Buck kept me mostly in line. He fulfilled that need I had for a close confidante without leading me into the mistake of cheating on my boyfriend. Although he was tempting, old Buck of the gorgeous ass. Don't think I didn't notice, because I did.

Once I was accepted into the graduate program at Northeastern, I rapidly used up what little money I'd saved. In a futile attempt to save up some more, I moved out of the 'burbs and into the tawdry student dorms. But mostly I hung out at Antoine's. With and without him. I buckled down, studied, went to class. Antoine and I worked hard, we fought hard, and we made up with great fervor.

He traveled more and more for work. Buck was always home. Managers have to be on duty twenty-four/seven. I could always rely on my pal to pass the joint, shoot the shit, make me laugh, and cheer me up.

Because it seemed like my life was slipping down

an invisible slope. When I sat around by myself and thought honestly about it, I was scared. The truth was, I was in over my head with both my financial commitments and my love life. Neither were providing me with the security I needed to make a life for myself in a big, anonymous, expensive city. And I was broke, in debt, lonely, and tired of the loneliness.

Then Antoine went to Australia to work on a big story. He rarely discussed investigations while they were still in the research stages, and a lot of what he worked on was, according to him, "top secret." Anti-bureaucratic diatribes from whistleblowers in government agencies. Juicy scoops from insiders on politicians with wandering eyes or dirty hands. Celeb gossip that could make or break a fragile reputation. To me, Tell All was yellow journalism. Not even journalism, just yellow blogging. But Antoine loved it. Espionage journalism, he called it. Freedom writing.

"There's no such thing as a lack of transparency, not anymore," he liked to say, "because all the information one could want is available to those who know how to find it." Tell All specialized in finding and documenting this kind of thing.

"Have hacker, will out," was another one of Antoine's mottos.

So I had no clue what he was working on when I drove him to Logan for his twenty-plus hours of flights to New York, Los Angles, and on to Honolulu and Sydney. I knew enough not to ask. We'd been arguing, mainly because he'd come home late on his last night in town. I'd already eaten the dinner I prepared for us— Gulf shrimp in garlic sauce, spinach salad with real bacon bits, chocolate walnut soufflé—and he stayed at the office past midnight?—and finally wandered downstairs. I was in Buck's apartment getting a contact high and watching a zombie movie when Antoine texted me from upstairs.

"He's bad for your work ethic, that guy," Antoine told me later, after what seemed to me nothing more than a courtesy fuck. "I need you to look after my place, not turn it into a crack den while I'm gone."

I laughed at that. "Fat chance," I said. "Guaranteed, the apartment under my care will be far neater than when you leave tomorrow morning."

"He's a bum. Do me a favor and promise me you'll stay away from Bearman while I'm away. Okay?"

What was I supposed to say to that? Okay, Daddy? So I pointlessly defended my personal taste in friends until things got ugly. We barely had time to squeeze in a make-up round of good-bye sex before it was time to hustle him off to the airport.

Antoine had asked me to take care of his apartment, water the plants and keep an eye on things. The day after he split, however, I moved in. Which didn't take much effort because I was traveling light. I'd been living light. Few worldly belongings beyond my laptop and a beloved cache of hardback books. Old novels, textbooks, some great biographies, which I read and reread for inspiration. People could make something of themselves and sometimes did. I also dragged in two battered suitcases stuffed with clothes, which I shoved into Antoine's closet. Then I went downstairs to tell Buck the good news. We celebrated with a couple of long necks and a blunt.

Living alone in my favorite part of Boston was far better than sharing a house in Newton with a bunch of twenty-somethings. And a huge change from sleeping on the floor in a tenement behind the university, a crummy rat-infested building that sat way too close to the train tracks. Plus, Jerry was just up the block. And my friend, the chronic bum, was right downstairs.

Things were okay for a few weeks. I behaved myself, mostly. The surfaces were stripped of clutter. The furniture shone with Lemon Pledge. The spider plants thrived. I tried not to worry when Antoine didn't call. Or text. Or email.

But after a month had passed without a word from him, I started to freak out. How could I track him down? I didn't know any of the people Antoine worked with, and the website had no centralized phone number. The company itself flew under the radar due to the sensitive nature of their investigative work. I wasn't surprised when nobody at the Tell All site responded to my emails inquiring after my missing boyfriend. I had no idea where the organization made its headquarters, if there even existed such a thing. Journalists and other employees lived all over the globe.

One desperate afternoon, I took the train into town. I'd never visited Antoine at his office, but I knew where it was located in a glass building on State Street. I rode a sleek elevator to the top floor and walked the carpeted hall to Suite 1400. The thick oak doors were locked and no one answered my heavy-handed knocks. I really hadn't expected anyone to, though. Whenever Antoine went undercover, he was gone.

This time, however, I'd begun to doubt he was coming back. At least, not to me. That's when I got angry. What? He'd dumped me just like that? Without even giving me the chance to defend myself?

Muthafuckah!

The downhill slide sped up significantly until I was rolling toward a hard landing at rock bottom. I skipped classes. I smoked too much reefer, got too drunk, hung out too often at Señor Cancun's. I went home with Jerry one too many times. I was burning the candle at both ends and up my own ass, and I knew it. So what did I do? I slept around even more. I drank and got high more often. I did whatever it took not to think about abandonment, loss, failure. Whenever I did ponder my sorry-ass situation, I blamed Antoine. My fucked-up life, I convinced myself, was a hundred percent his fault.

After the second month of no contact, I considered Antoine a nonperson. He was dead to me. I regarded myself as the rightful heir to everything he'd left behind.

So, yes, I was a fucking mess. In truth, I was depressed. After all, my lover had blown me off. Without explanation, he'd just gone and disappeared on me. Poof. So, to recompense, I reminded myself between crying and drinking bouts that all was not lost. Look how much collateral I had. I had his fun little car, his nice little apartment, all his expensive furnishings. I had his wall art, his tennis racquets, his cuff links. Antoine had some really nice shit. All of which remained quite comforting until the bills started piling up. Mine *and* my missing boyfriend's.

I'd taken over the rent, the electric bills, the cable and phones. I paid for the water, the kitchen sink declogging, the new showerhead in the bathroom. I did what I could until I couldn't anymore. It didn't take long. Soon enough, my financial problems forced me to drop out of grad school. I pieced together menial jobs to supplement the diminished tutoring work. Pet sitting, dog walking, babysitting. I had a paper route for a month or two. Then I collected cans, turned them in for the deposit money.

The shit got real. Real quick.

One night, I clicked around online, looking for new money-making ideas. I needed a steady source of income a woman could rely on if she had more desperation than scruples. After about five minutes, I found my answer.

I went to my favorite bartender for a connection. Jerry didn't approve, but he understood. He hooked me up with Cedrick7Z. After I met with my pimp-to-be at the John Hancock Jazz Bar, we trekked out to the black Benz in the parking garage. The sleek leather interior smelled like juniper berries and sperm. I auditioned, I got the part. I sucked, though, and that is never good enough.

I didn't exactly miss Antoine in my life. We'd been a bad match. We were too distant, too separate, to make the intimacy matter. But I lost something of value when he disappeared. And I also lost the desire to find someone who mattered. Someone who might stick around. After the rude blow off from Antoine, I wanted my love light and easy. I knew how love worked. So I wouldn't ever expect to love somebody long and hard.

The new me was a sex entrepreneur. I would replace what Antoine, what *life* had taken from me, with quick cash. And plenty of it.

****

After I showered and tossed up a green salad—boy, that lettuce was old; but who can spot the mold on romaine?—it was time to head into town for the gig. I wriggled into a pair of black jeans and a dark T-shirt, grabbed my collapsible backpack, and went out to find the Mini. I remembered parking it a few blocks off Huntington in an iffier section of the neighborhood.

As soon as I rounded the corner, I could see exactly what had happened. The hood was still propped open.

My battery was gone. Again.

"Muthafuckahs!" I yelled, startling two women pushing double strollers. Both blonde, bobbed, Spandexed and trim, they turned as one to give me the hairy eyeball. The Bobbsey Twins with their double-trouble twin sets. Why did kids always come in pairs these days? Wasn't one little regret enough? Same with dogs. Used to be you could own a solo pet. Now you had to lay claim to a yapping herd.

"Fucking douchebag battery thieves," I explained to the moms, who hurried away as fast as their neon-hued Nikes would carry them.

I speed-dialed the crew to make a new plan. Our simple fuck 'n' grab just got more complicated.

Chapter Eight

"I hope she can pull this off. She's not making much of an effort," Mary-Ann commented. "She's acting so cold. Colder than that piece of wild Alaskan salmon she ordered. Bet it's still sitting there. On her fifty-dollar plate. He's never gonna take her to bed. Not if she keeps up the ice queen routine."

"Shh," Ginger said. "He's stopped bugging her to eat the salmon. Now he's asking her to go somewhere else."

I put down the coffee pot and hustled into the living room to listen. My phone was propped up on an end table, volume on high. First thing I would buy with tonight's profits would be the kind of spyware Antoine had shown me. Some of the audio-video gadgets he had access to were James Bond cool. That this kind of high-tech equipment was available on the open market was so awesome. Anyone could be a spy, even a bunch of fuckgirls like us.

"What's he saying?" I asked.

Their dialogue was hard to understand. The mark was situated too far from the phone and background noises overwhelmed most of what he said. They were dining outside, which diffused their voices even more. A soft but continuous slapping sound, presumably from the sea beyond their table, made it impossible to fully understand what anyone was saying.

A male, most likely a waiter, said, "Thank you, sir," then the voice petered out to an indecipherable drone. Barry fucking Manilow sang softly about lost love. A woman cackled. All of this overwhelmed whatever Wendell Hawthorne the Third was imparting to his date.

I returned to Mr. Coffee and poured myself a good jolt. I was worried Skipper would be unable to seal the deal and get him down and out. Her silence was not a good sign. Maybe her nerves and her frigidity were interfering with her natural seduction capabilities. A shame.

"He wants to go to some apartment," Mary-Ann called out. "In Southie, of all places."

"I don't know my way around that part of—"

"Shh." Ginger held up a hand to quiet us.

We shut up. I tiptoed back to the living room to listen. We were at a critical moment, and our timing would be crucial. Mary-Ann had her father's truck parked outside my place, ready to roll, but we'd had to wait for him to get home from a meeting. He was late, so we were late. In fact, we didn't have time to scoot into town to monitor Skipper at the restaurant. Instead, we were waiting at my place for the happy couple to agree on their after-dinner plans. We would head out once we knew the coordinates and keep an ear on her there. Wherever *there* turned out to be.

Skipper and the mark had lingered over their expensive meal, chatting. Actually, he had been doing all the chatting. She was mostly listening. Or pretending to listen, like all good girls must learn to do with their men. I hoped she was at least putting on a Dating Barbie face, looking enthralled. And sexy as hell. Hot to trot. Whatever it would take to get him into a bedroom somewhere and knock him the fuck out.

Wherever Skipper ended up after dinner, we'd park outside and wait for her call.

The mark mumbled something. We all leaned in and gave one another puzzled looks. What the hell was the guy saying?

Then, there she was. Speaking carefully, enunciating each word. For our benefit.

"You're asking me to go with you to your apartment? In South Boston? But I thought you said you lived in a nice big house in Malden."

He responded. Grumble, mumble. Whatever Wendell was saying sounded like mumbledegook to me. When I slurped some coffee, my hand shook. Excitement, fear, maybe both.

"What's he saying?" I asked again.

"He says he has a friend's place for the night. On N Street," Ginger translated. "Or M, maybe. Shh."

Nobody spoke. We were listening, barely breathing.

"I'll need an address," Skipper said. "I like to know where I'm going. In case I don't like it when I get there." She laughed. Nervously. She wasn't being very smooth. She sounded like a virgin. Cool, distrustful, wary.

The Third spoke quietly. Too quietly. I pictured him holding Skipper's hand, playing with her long fingers, his heart bouncing around as he attempted to woo her into going somewhere they could be alone. So he could ravish her.

Little did he know, he was the one who would be flat on his back on the bed. Chewed up and spit out.

Skipper spoke up again, her voice clear, calm, controlled. "Sure, I'd like that. Let me just freshen up. Be back in a minute."

We looked at one another. That was the signal. Skipper was going to head for the privacy of a ladies room stall and hit us with the address. I grabbed the phone as the three of us ran out of my apartment.

Somewhere en route to the street, on our way to the truck, the call dropped.

"Shit, I lost her."

"Call her back," Ginger said.

"Wait. What if she's with him? Still sitting at the table?" Mary-Ann unlocked the doors to her dad's massive black truck with a loud beep. "Just wait 'til she calls us from the bathroom. Meantime, we'll head in. To Southie."

We climbed into the long-bed, and Mary-Ann started it up, the powerful headlights illuminating the four-seater cab. My phone did not ring. I took the risk and called her back. My call went straight to message.

I hung up. "Shit."

"I hope she can pull this off," Mary-Ann said for the umpteenth time as she edged the Dodge Ram into the heavy traffic on Centre Street. "She said like two words the entire meal."

"She hates the guy, obviously," Ginger said from the back seat. "He don't care, though. He still wants to get his dick wet." She spoke from experience, her pink bow mouth distorted with disgust. "She better knock that guy out soon as they get to the apartment, or he'll be in her before she knows what hit her. And I do mean *hit* her."

I was pretty sure this was coming from somewhere

other than the present situation. Ginger was heading down the wrong road with her all-men-are-violent-pigs kind of thinking, and I wanted to cut her off at the pass. "He's more intimidated by her than she is by him, Ginger. Don't worry. Skipper can keep him on his knees for twenty minutes or so. By then, he'll be too groggy to force any issues."

Yeah, I sounded sure of myself, confident in Skipper and the plan for tonight's heist. But underneath my bravado, I was worried. I didn't like being disconnected. It felt like we'd abandoned Skipper when she might need us most.

I rolled down the window and hung my head out. The air was muggy, like it might rain, but the warm wind felt good on my face. God, I was revved up. No wonder Antoine was so addicted to his work. Spying was an incredible adrenaline pumper. Really got the imagination zooming.

"We'll see who ends up on their knees once she gets back to his place," Ginger said in a dark voice. "Pedal down, Mary-Ann, or we'll get stuck at this fricking light."

Mary-Ann looked in the rearview mirror. "Relax, girl. I'm not getting any traffic violations tonight. Not in my dad's truck. He'll kill me." She tossed her ponytail, slowed for the yellow light. "She hasn't even called us back. She's probably still in the ladies room. Making him wait. Giving us plenty of time to get to Southie, stake out the area."

I pulled my overcaffeinated head back into the cab. "I wish she'd fucking call. The three of us can spread out, patrol both M and N Street, but it'll be too easy to miss her. I want to talk to her before she goes inside that apartment. I want the address, and I need to know she's cool with this next step."

"If she's not, she's off the team," Mary-Ann said. "I need this gig to work out. I really do. I can't be out all night with my dad's truck, come home empty handed."

"Skipper'll do fine—" I started to say.

"Don't be such a selfish bitch," Ginger interjected. "When was the last time *you* had to fuck some guy you didn't like?"

"Never," Mary-Ann admitted. "I always like them. Until *after* I fuck them."

We laughed.

None of us said much after that. The streets were hectic, full of weekend partiers and crowds leaving the symphony, the area restaurants and bars. The air smelled like curry, men's cologne, and stale beer. Mary-Ann drove slowly, easing us through the congestion and on through downtown. We passed Fort Point Channel and were soon navigating the tight streets of South Boston.

We kept waiting for the phone to ring. It didn't. I tried again and got nowhere. We had lost her.

When we arrived at the turn for M, a pretty street lined with classic brownstones facing a brightly lit park, Mary-Ann idled at a stop sign. She fiddled with her bangs. "Now what?"

I wished I knew. But I didn't, so I improvised. "Park on the street. Down there, across from the park. But not under the field lights."

Mary-Ann did as I'd suggested. Once she'd situated us in the semi-darkness, she turned off the engine. Crickets buzz-sawed the night air, and tall oak trees rustled in the soft wind. You could smell the ocean, its richly scented brine. The sidewalks were desolate, as were the softball fields, the basketball courts, the long sweeps of cultivated grass. A feral cat stalked across the playground, its belly dragging on the sand.

Still no word from Skipper.

"Let's make sure we don't miss her," I said. "We can split up, walk around, watch out for the two of them getting out of his car." I had no idea whether this would work, but what else could we do? "If you see them, note the address and text the rest of us. We'll meet back here."

Fortunately, we were in the nice part of Southie. And it was early yet, only ten-thirty. I went to the far end of M and stood between two black SUVs, monitoring the line of well-kept brownstones for any signs of activity. I tried to look like I was busy texting someone, in case any neighbors thought me suspicious. A man in a trench coat walked past with a big black poodle and a tiny white fluff-mop of a dog. They ignored me.

I walked down the block and leaned against a late model BMW, pretending to fiddle with my phone. In front garden after garden, the crocuses were in bloom and, here and there, brightly colored tulips. Sea breezes fluttered the petals on the dogwood trees. It was a gorgeous night in South Boston. Too bad I was unable to enjoy it.

My phone vibrated, and I retrieved the text. Ginger. *Chick has nested, meet @ truck.*

I walked quickly back to the truck.

"They're up that way, like six blocks," she reported

to us while we stood in the shadows by Mary-Ann's gas-guzzler. Ginger was out of breath, her curls damp with sweat. "Got the house number, too." She laughed. "He had his arm around her when they went up the steps, and she was leaning on him like she was into it."

"Good girl," I said. "I knew Skipper would come through."

We were all smiling, excited. Our plan was working.

I pointed to the truck. "So now we move. We can park across the street and wait for her call. The minute he's knocked out, that's when she'll call us."

We climbed back in the long-bed, and Ginger directed us to an open space near the small, neat building she'd seen them enter. On the second floor, a few windows were lit up. We made guesses as to which one might be Wendell's friend's living room. Or bedroom. After a few minutes of joshing around, we settled in to wait.

The sky suddenly opened up, and rain splattered against the truck. Mary-Ann rolled up the windows, and we lounged in the warm truck cab, chatting quietly. Thunder ripped the sky a new one, and lightning sewed it up again. Time crawled along, dragging us with it.

I'd thought she would take around twenty minutes, maybe half an hour, before calling us. We would scurry up to the apartment door, and she could buzz us inside. Then we'd be able to lend an assist with whatever grab was there for the grabbing.

"Any minute now, Skipper will call," I said a little after eleven o'clock.

But I was wrong.

Chapter Nine

By the time we finally heard from her, I'd been edging into panic. I had started to advocate for intervention. We could go up to the building and ring a bunch of doorbells until somebody buzzed us inside. We could save her from whatever mess we'd gotten the poor frigid girl into. What if Hawthorne was some kind of weirdo soft cock? What if he'd surprised her somehow and tied her up? Taken away her phone, her dignity? Pushed her around, hurt her? My imagination was on a tear. I could really scare myself sometimes.

It was after midnight, and my limbs were shaking from pent-up nervous tension. The street was quiet and, except for a svelte woman in a short black skirt and thigh-high black boots—Got hooker?—who had come and gone from the building where Skipper was still doing god knows what, there'd been surprisingly few signs of life. An occasional car whisked by, a handful of dog walkers, a few well-heeled residents rushing into their well-heeled homes. One lone drunk, an old man with a brown bag and a sad stumble, had reeled past and veered into the park. The glaring lack of activity was fueling my angst. It was Friday night. Where were all the rest of the drunken Irishmen this part of Boston was famous for?

Still in the bars, of course.

I was about to pile out of the truck to go harass

some Southie residents by pressing on their door buzzers when the text arrived. The beep made me jump, and I knocked my head against the window. *Ouch.*

"Oh, my god," Ginger yelped from the backseat. "Is she okay?"

"Fucking finally," Mary-Ann said. "My ass has gone flat. Flat and bum numb."

"She texted me the address," I told them. "Says she'll be out front. We'll need to nab her the second she comes through that door."

Mary-Ann started up the truck and rolled down the windows. The rain had stopped, and the fresh air tasted delicious. I breathed deep and hard. My heart was running up and down the steps of my chest like a madman at the John Hancock building. What was taking Skipper so long?

The front door was lipstick red with a real brass knocker. A lion's head. Classy. We all stared at it, willing it to open. Finally, it did.

"There she is. Fucking finally," Mary-Ann whispered and stuck her arm out the window, beckoning.

Skipper ran across the street. Rumpled and barefoot, she had her stiletto heels in one hand, the other pressed against her mouth. Her leather purse did not look stuffed with bling, and the backpack was nowhere in sight.

Ginger leaned across the seat to crack open the back door while I watched the apartment building for any signs of life. Nobody else came out of it. The street sat there, looking perfect, empty of life. The night remained silent, thick, full of its own darkness.

When she climbed into the back seat, Skipper burst

out laughing. "Oh, my god, what kind of a rig is this? Real subtle, four women in a four by four."

Ginger said, "Shh," and Mary-Ann rolled up the windows.

I started in, sounding like the nervous mother of a teenager who'd arrived home late from a date. "Where the hell have you been? We were so worried about you!"

She kept giggling. I wanted to slap her until she stopped. But I needed directions, and only Skipper could give them to me. "Hey, chill out. Can we get the hell out of Southie now? Or do we need to go inside with you and get ourselves some swag?"

Skipper's eyes ran with mirthful tears. Sure, the truck was not the best getaway vehicle. It was too bulky, way too obvious for our needs, but really. Was it *that* hilarious?

"What the fuck, Skip?" I said, pissy. "We've been out here all night. Why didn't you call? What happened to the plan?"

She made a strange grimace and shifted in her seat. Tenderly, like her bottom parts hurt. Uh-oh.

"Did that fucker hurt you?" I asked.

Skipper laughed again. "Drive, Mary-Ann. Now. I promise I'll tell you everything on the way. Oh, my god, what a fucked up night. And I've got to get this thing out of my..." She raised one lovely eyebrow. "What if I told you guys I have twenty-five thousand dollars in my vagina?"

Her cocky grin was contagious. Ginger snickered. Mary-Ann ground hard in reverse, then lurched into drive. She pumped a fist. "Awright, sistah."

I gave Skipper a slow smile. "I'd say you had a

golden snatch, girlfriend."

"Gold? Oh, you got that right. Plus, it's diamond studded," she answered. "And sharp. So please get me home, girls. I can't wait to slide that thing outta there. And share the wealth."

When Mary-Ann floored it, we all laughed. Yes, indeed, our snatch and grab gang had done it. And on our first attempt.

It had been less than a week, and already we'd executed our first successful heist.

****

On the cruise into town, while sitting in traffic by the Boston Common and all the way down Mass. Ave. toward Skipper's place in Somerville, she shared the details of her date with Wendell Hawthorne the Third. Starting with the bling she'd managed to take with her after she left him on the king-sized bed on M Street.

"Same Rolex he had on the night we all met him. A beaut. Left him there, snoring. Man was out cold," she said, "and only a quarter of his drink was gone. The Third, he's such a wuss." She sat forward in her seat, shifting her loins carefully. "And a scumbag of the highest order."

"All attorneys are scum," Mary-Ann said with a shrug. "But usually they're loaded. So why only the watch? He didn't have anything else worth taking?" She braked, and we all snapped up and back in our seats. "Sorry. Didn't see that guy on the bicycle until the last minute. Asshole."

We passed a kid on a mountain bike. He was wearing a white hoodie. I decided to ignore it this time. Must be a new banger style or some subgang colors thing. The boy didn't look up as we sailed by.

"I thought about stripping the place, taking some of the awesome, and I mean fucking *awesome*, artwork off the walls. But really, it was such a bachelor pad. White on white, brick walls, open space, loft bed. A studio. But huge, with a nice mahogany bar and dynamite electronics. I didn't see much that would fit in a backpack. And I wasn't about to lug the sixty-inch TV down the stairs."

I supported her decision while she paused for breath. "Right, of course. We need to stick to jewelry, cash, small goods. No artwork. Too hard to fence. No big stuff, no televisions, fancy espresso machines. No bulk. Nothing that shows."

"Well, I sure got that right. Nothing showing over here." She laughed. "Oh, and speaking of cash."

Skipper reached into her purse, then leaned forward to hand me a thick wad of bills. "Not sure how much is there, but I left him a ten spot. So maybe he'll think he spent it all on dinner at that fat-ass WASP restaurant."

"Doubt that," Mary-Ann said. "He'll know who took it. Soon as he sees it's gone."

"But he might not know it was me who lightened him up."

I stopped participating in the conversation. My eyes were glued to the pile of cash sitting in my lap. Dazzled, I spread the bills across my thighs in a fan shape and stared at the twenties, the fifties, the hundreds, guestimating. Over a thousand, for sure.

"Doubt that," Mary-Ann said again. "So what happened at dinner? Couldn't hear a thing he was saying. Too much ambient noise. Could hear you perfectly. Until you hung up on us." She stopped for a red light, gave Skipper a hard stare in the rearview mirror. "Why'd you hang up?"

I looked up, then back to my lap. I was counting the bills. The cash felt smooth, like fat silk. My hands caressed it. There was something about a stack of freshly stolen money that really turned me on. My heart pounded a little reggae tune in my ears. I almost had an orgasm just from running my fingers across the loot.

"Okay, here's what happened before we went to his place. Which is, by the way, his. Not a friend's, as he pretended. It's a *pied-à-terre* he keeps in the city for sexing it up. The way he lured me there, that was just one of his many lies." Her voice sharpened. "Guy's a scumbag. He fucks around on his family, and his clients are all gangsters. Shady bankers, corporate polluters, mobbed up creeps with RICO raps, other lowlife types. Southie is like a second home to him, because that's where his client base is. Man has some really questionable business ethics."

I thought about Jerry's mob friends. Cedrick7Z. Me. Us. Look who was talking about moral values.

"Too bad we weren't out in Malden at his family estate. I could've cleaned out his ass," Skipper said with a grin.

"Nasty," Ginger said. "I don't like the visual on that one."

They started laughing, making crude jokes. I was half-listening, my heart jumping up and down while I recounted the money. Two thousand eight hundred and sixty-nine dollars. More money than I'd seen in a long time. My cut wouldn't be huge, but still, it was a start. Plus, we had the Rolex. Not bad for a night's work.

We were approaching the Mass. Ave. bridge. I

tucked the wad of cash into the pocket of my sweatshirt. "Okay, Skip. Give us your address so Mary-Ann can plug it into the GPS. Then I want you to tell your story. In order. From the minute you met up with Wendell Hawthorne the Third to the second you spotted Mary-Ann's hand waving from the truck window."

"I'm in Davis Square," she told Mary-Ann, who took a quick right to cross the river into Cambridge. "When you get there, I'll direct you. I don't want my address in anyone's computer."

Smart girl.

"Stop here," she barked.

Mary-Ann pulled over and parked, engine running. I thought Skipper was going to be sick when she rolled her window all the way down and leaned out. Instead, she tossed something out. It landed with a plop in a big metal garbage can.

"Temp phone," she told us. "Now he can't call me. Ever again."

The blow off of our first mark was now complete.

Mary-Ann roared ahead into the city of Cambridge. Ah, life! The narrow streets thronged with people, bar-goers and nightclubbers, joggers and skateboarders, wanderers and lovers of all persuasions. I admired the day-glo pink, green, and blue hair and the wild tattoos, all brightly lit from street lamps and clustering neon signs. My angst rapidly subsided.

"Tell," I instructed Skipper. And she did.

Dinner had been a stuffy affair with too many spoons on crisp white linen tablecloths. The diners there were a dull crowd, mostly elderly couples in their Sunday best eating onion soup and baked trout. The restaurant was old class, the type of place Hawthorne's cronies would never go on a Friday night. The type of place a married guy hides his date. The food was bland, the sort of overcooked fare the Brahmins eat after most of their teeth fall out. But the view, Skipper told us, was breathtaking.

They'd sat at an elegant table out on the deck, watching the moonlight dance on the bay. The tide washed up against barnacled pilings, which accounted for the constant slapping sound in the background. The splash of the sea had interfered with our ability to overhear what Skipper's mark was blathering on about during dinner. She'd figured it was hard for us to hear, but there was nothing she could do.

Skipper informed us we'd been lucky on that score, too. The Third was one of those narcissistic success stories, the boring top dogs who love nothing more than the sound of their own voice. He asked few questions, spoke mainly of his accomplishments in the stock market, in playing squash against fellow attorneys, and in winning suits for his clients who, according to Skipper, were a bunch of wealthy villains.

"He's a *criminal* lawyer marketing himself as a civil lawyer," she said. "A game-playing, moneygrubbing scumbag. I couldn't wait to knock him out so I didn't have to listen to any more of his boring bullshit. If I could've gotten away with it, I would've doctored the Bordeaux and left him there, face-planted in his linguini with clams."

But she'd hung in there, smiling brightly, nibbling on her cold salmon and, later, almond cheesecake. She'd been nervous, like we suspected, and sick with dread. How would she be able to let this man touch her? The thought of it made her skin crawl. However, she doubted he'd even noticed her silent brooding.

"He was so into himself, he hardly saw me. I was the captive audience, nothing more."

"Been there, done that," Ginger said.

"Amen, sistah," Mary-Ann added.

We all knew what Skipper was talking about. What woman hasn't experienced the feeling of being invisible, or at least interchangeable, when out on a date with a self-involved man? That's why we usually fell so hard for the guys who actually seemed to care. When we could find one. Which wasn't very often.

"The wine, however, was totally excellent," Skipper said with a laugh. "In fact, it would've been a delightful night if it had just been me, the ocean, and that robust bottle of Château Latour."

After the meal was over and while she sipped an espresso, the mark made his move. He invited her to see his friend's studio on M Street. Just drop by for a minute, look at the artwork, then he would drive her home. Yes, she'd said, why not? She would love to go to his friend's apartment in South Boston.

Skipper described how she got a chunk of cheesecake stuck in her throat and she'd had to ignore the waves of nausea. What if he jumped on her the moment they walked into the foyer? She found the man so reprehensible, so repulsive, would she be able to resist the urge to give him a swift karate kick to the balls?

Somehow, she managed to convey a desire to spend time alone with him, so he signaled the waiter and requested the check. Then things got dicey. Skipper's phone disconnected when she got up to go to the ladies room, then she couldn't find a signal. Some cell tower issue, one of those technical glitches. Her nausea increased, but she sucked it up, determined to carry on with the plan.

In the fluorescent lit bathroom, she splashed her temples with cool water and took deep, meditative breaths. At this point, Skipper had talked herself into remaining calm. After all, she could certainly handle the man on her own. He was all talk. She, on the other hand, had been all action her entire life. She thought we'd been able to overhear the address where he would be taking her after dinner. So, with us parked out front, she figured she'd be safe enough in an apartment in South Boston. Safe enough to attempt the next step. Drinks for two, sleep for one.

"I looked at myself in the unforgiving mirror in that empty bathroom," Skipper said to us. "I looked deep into my own aging face."

I had turned around in my seat to listen to Skipper's recounting. The headlights of passing cars occasionally lit up her smooth, lovely face. Women. We are such harsh critics of our physical selves.

"And I said to myself, 'Girl, you got a few good years left to make it on your looks. Then all that goes away. So go out there and do what you have to do while you're still able. And be grateful for the opportunity. Not everyone gets one like this.'"

I nodded. So did Ginger and Mary-Ann. We knew how she felt. What woman doesn't think about her built-in obsolescence? Once you hit twenty, twenty-one, sometimes that's all you *can* think about.

"I'd been stealing glances at his Rolex for the three hours we'd been sitting across from one another. That thing was so bright and shiny, sparkly as the bay in the moonlight. If it hadn't been for that lovely piece of bling, I doubt I would've been able to sit through that torturous dinner. So I promised myself I'd be leaving the man behind. Soon, real soon. And when I did, the watch would be in my possession." She grinned. "Didn't know I'd be carrying it where the sun don't shine, though."

We laughed.

"Better to be toting a Rolex in there than some douchebag's sperm," Ginger said.

When we all stopped giggling, Skipper continued with her story.

After the valet brought around Hawthorne's cherry-red convertible Austin-Healey, Skipper perked up. She loved the car. He opened her door for her, slid the top down, and they took off. The night wind cooled them all the way into South Boston. Wendell had remained blessedly silent, so Skipper enjoyed the ride. M Street was impressive, too, the old brownstones lined up like dowagers across from the lush green park. All the trappings—apartment, car, wine, restaurant, these things were seductive. But the man? The man was shit.

He parked in an alley behind the townhomes. As a precaution, she assumed, but she wasn't sure who he was hiding from since his wife was at home in Malden with the children. Cute kids, too, she'd seen photos. Four cute little blondes and a pretty, honey-haired wife.

"Muthafuckah," Mary-Ann said, then took a sharp left when Skipper told her to. "He knocks her up, ruins her vagina with four babies, then goes out and gets himself young pussy. Hate men like that."

"You must hate all men, then," Ginger remarked dryly. "Go on, Skipper. What happened at the apartment?"

He'd invited her to relax on the white leather couch while he mixed up a cocktail shaker of martinis. Skipper set her purse on the kitchen counter so she could access the knockout drug hidden inside. Then she took over the cocktail preparation by saying, "I want you to go into the bedroom and get ready for me, Wen. I'll bring in the drinks in a moment."

He kissed her hard on the lips, grabbing her head in a kind of wrestler's lock. He smelled like clams, like garlic, like someone else's husband. She had to put everything into that kiss, everything she did not feel for the man who had his hands all over her backside, kneading her ass greedily with his hard, cold fingers. She pulled away as soon as she could and patted him on the butt, as if to say, *Off with you and Mama will be right along with the goodies.* He grinned, headed for the stairs to the loft.

"His smell, it filled up my head. I had to push it out in order to have room for my thoughts," Skipper said. "I needed to focus on what I had to do, and be quick and quiet about it. You could hear everything in that apartment. It's like one big, open room. There's no carpet to absorb the sound."

While he clomped around overhead getting ready for her to bend to his will, Skipper took charge. The drugging went smoothly. She removed from her purse the ziplock plastic bag containing an innocent looking herbal tonic bottle. Then she added one full eye-dropper of Liquid E to one of the martinis. After eating the olives out of the second glass, to make sure she could tell the two apart, she grabbed her purse and headed for the stairs. She carried the drinks up the narrow staircase to the loft.

When she walked into the master suite, Wen was lying on his back on the bed. Naked. Stroking himself.

"Small and unimpressive," she told us. "Typical WASP attorney cock."

We laughed, but our mirth was touched with bitterness and scorn. After listening to a man brag all night about how wonderful he is, what woman has not been disappointed when confronted with the naked truth? Why oh why do we get seduced by their egos instead of falling in love with their hearts?

"Collecting my wits, I was able to smile at Wen and say, 'I see you're all ready for me, baby.'" Skipper laughed. "Hardest sentence I ever spoke. So icky and trite."

At this point in the story, Skipper stopped to direct Mary-Ann to the house. After we'd pulled up in front, she told Mary-Ann to park in the driveway next to the duplex. No parking problem in Davis Square, I noticed with not a little envy. We sat there in the truck, windows down, night air still and sweet. We sat there, enthralled by Skipper's experiences and her reactions to what occurred.

"I handed him the doctored drink, then went around to the foot of the bed. I sipped mine just a little, stepped out of my shoes. He downed a good gulp, set the glass on the night table. The whole time he was watching me with those shifty eyes of his, so I drank a little more and giggled. Hoping he'd follow suit, keep drinking. But he didn't. He played with his sad sack dick and said, 'Take your clothes off, darlin'. Nice and slow.' I said, 'I'm finishing my martini first. You go ahead with what you're doing, and I'll watch.'"

That's when they heard the front door open. And a woman's voice call out, "Wen? I know you're here. I saw your car out back."

"Shit. My girlfriend," he whispered. "Can you hide in the closet for a few minutes? I'll send her home."

He jumped up, quickly slipping his Ralph Lauren boxers over a deflating erection. "Up here, babe," he yelled. "Hang on, I'll be right down. I must've fallen asleep. Reading."

Skipper took her glass, her shoes, and her purse and stepped into the walk-in. The room-size closet didn't have much in it, so she had plenty of space. Several teak bureaus lined one long wall, next to empty hat racks and shoe racks. Hangers on poles held a line of oxford shirts and several men's suits. Everything looked like it would fit The Third just perfectly. Obviously, the place was his, not some friend's studio.

"I sat on the floor and leaned back against the wall. Drank the rest of my drink. My very first martini. Ever. I liked it. I tried texting you guys, but I couldn't get a signal. Downstairs, the two of them were arguing. I couldn't hear what they were saying, just the raised voices. I was hoping he wouldn't suddenly pass out. Every few minutes I checked the signal again, but my phone was dead. So I just sat there, waiting."

"Who was she?" Mary-Ann asked.

"Not sure. His girlfriend, I guess, like he said. Or one of them, maybe. But I have no details. Once they came upstairs and he started fucking her, they didn't say a word to one another until they were done."

I could see her eyes glistening in the darkness of the truck cab. Her voice hardened. She was angry. I would have been, too.

105

"I sat there, listening to them go at it. I felt disgusting, like some kind of twisted voyeur. But I had no choice. I was forced to hear him slam and slam and slam into her. And I will admit to you girls, I was so fucking glad it wasn't me. When he finally came, after what seemed like a goddam hour of wailing on her, he yelled her name. At least, I think it was her name. Daphne. Then instantly, and I mean *instantly*, he fell asleep. I could hear him snoring. From inside the closet!"

I was remembering the booted blonde who had come and gone from the building while we were waiting out front in the truck. Hadn't that woman walked down the street to another building and gone up the stairs? Was that her, the girlfriend? Daphne? Was she a neighbor? Neighborhood hooker?

"How much time passed? I mean, do you think the E finally hit him?" I asked.

"Maybe. Or maybe he's just a selfish prick. Which is what Daphne said. 'Selfish cocksucker' was her exact wording. Then she swore a lot while she stormed around the room, getting dressed, I assume, and stomped down the stairs."

"Can't blame her," Mary-Ann said. "Hate guys who fuck and sleep. Assholes."

"Don't all men fuck and sleep?" Ginger asked. I wasn't sure if she was kidding. She wasn't smiling.

"When I heard the front door slam, I stood up and walked out of the closet. He was still out, sawing the big logs. So I went downstairs and rinsed out the martini glasses, put them away. When I tried the phone again, I finally caught the signal. That's when I texted you guys."

I nodded. We'd need a more reliable way of staying in contact during future heists. Cell phone towers were not all that dependable. I reached in my pocket and petted the cash. Was this why they called it "petty" cash?

"I thought I'd better go back upstairs and check him one last time, just to make sure he was okay," Skipper said. "Man was dead to the world, hadn't moved a muscle. So he was either sound asleep or he'd been drugged enough. Either way, he was down for the count."

Skipper shifted in her seat, reached out to grab the door handle. "You know the rest," she said.

"But what about the watch?" I asked. "Why hide it? Why didn't you just put it in the purse with the cash?"

She laughed. "I snatched the freaking Rolex right away. As soon as he went downstairs to deal with his girlfriend, I grabbed it off the night table. There was no way I was going to leave that apartment without it. By that time, I'd decided the watch was all I was taking. If he got rid of her like he said he would, I was going to act angry that he had a girlfriend and storm out. But just in case he noticed his watch was missing, got suspicious, wanted to check my purse, I hid it. Somewhere I was gonna make sure he didn't get the opportunity to look."

Wow. Gutsy! I admired her spunk and ingenuity. This woman could definitely think on her size eleven feet.

"And the cash?" I asked her. "When did you cop that?"

Skipper cracked her door open. "Once I knew he

wasn't about to wake up anytime soon, I had the urge to check his wallet. So I plucked his pants off the wing chair where he'd carefully laid out his clothes. I was at the very least going to grab cab fare. In case you guys weren't out front for whatever reason."

I nodded. Of course. She had to split as soon as possible. But checking for cash was a must on every successful gig.

"Girls," I said. "Lesson here. Always go through the wallet once the mark goes down. Important."

I would show them just how important later when I revealed how much was in tonight's cash grab.

"And that's when I saw the photo of the wife and four little towheads," Skipper continued. "Such a sweet looking family. Why does he have so little respect for them? For his so-called girlfriend? For the law? For other people in general, like me in particular? Just thinking about him stretched out on the bed with his sorry dick in his hand...that just made me mad. Wanging away at somebody he's involved with romantically or sexually or something, all huff and puff, knowing I'm like fifteen feet away, trapped in his freaking closet? God, what kind of animal does shit like that? Selfish cocksucker." She paused for a moment to calm herself. "It felt so good to rip the man off."

She swung open the truck door and climbed down slowly. Then she leaned inside again. "Come on in, you guys. I want to show you the fucking watch. It's awesome."

"*Fucking* watch? That's funny. Considering the current location," Mary-Ann said as she hopped out of the truck, locking the doors with a quick beep of the remote.

I was stuck on the word *awesome*. Because awesome described it perfectly. The watch *and* the cash. Our first snatch and grab had proven to be fucking *awesome*. Or was it a grab *in* snatch?

Hand still clasping the cash, I skipped across the front lawn after my crew. Maybe I'd felt like a loser for too long. Being poor all my life, dropping out of Northeastern due to financial hardship, owing so much in student loans and facing a depressing lack of decent employment prospects. Working dumb jobs and tutoring rich kids who had no idea how hard it was to get by. Losing Antoine the way I had. Selling my body, my mouth, that one horrible, humiliating night. From odd jobs to blowjobs, maybe all the years of struggle and loss had done damage to my self-esteem. Maybe I was vulnerable to crime, to the neurochemical high that came from taking back from the system that had done me so wrong.

Actually, I'm not sure why I got off so much on our first score. But right then, scurrying across the damp grass behind my dynamite girl gang, my pocket stuffed with more than two thousand dollars, my friend's twat with top-flight bling, I was flying. Oh, yeah, I felt pretty fucking awesome myself.

Lilac bushes lined the walkway that led to the hulking two-story Victorian where Skipper rented an attic apartment. The aroma was heady, sweetening the night even more. In the splashing moonlight, fluttery purple petals glistened with a silvery white coating. When I squinted my eyes at them, my crew sparkled, too. It was beautiful. It was like the world had been dipped in glitter.

Chapter Ten

When my mother called the next afternoon, Ginger was still asleep on the divan. I took my phone out front and sat on the stoop. The sky was cloudy, the wind briny.

It had been several weeks since we'd talked, and it was good to hear her voice. "I sent you a check yesterday," she confided. "Don't tell Kent." I heard her suck in a breath, let it out slowly. I pictured the cloud of blue smoke curling from her full mouth and her waving it away from her short auburn hair. "He's been bitchy lately. His golf game is off."

"Mom, you shouldn't send me any more money. I've told you that. I'm fine," I lied. Of course, she knew I was lying. She always knew.

"You sleep with that cute man downstairs yet?" My mother giggled. She was kind of in love with Buck, mainly because she'd married a dried up wisp of a guy with the sex appeal of a twirl of lemon rind. "Chuck?"

In previous conversations, I'd told her about my friendship with Buck. She thought I needed to end the palling around and get down to business. My mother did not have male friends. She had lovers, and the occasional husband.

"Buck, Mom. And no, we're still friends. But listen to this. I just scored some freelance work, so that income is gonna prop me up for a while. I like the work, too. It's…different."

"That's great, honey. Glad to hear it." She didn't pry into my work life. Just my love life. "What do you hear from Antoine? He still in Sydney?"

I didn't want her to worry about me. Really, there was nothing she could do to fix the situation, and she'd only get upset, complain about feeling helpless, and try to think up ways to save me from my loneliness. I couldn't bear that. So I hadn't told her yet that Antoine and I were… What? Estranged? I wasn't lying, just evading. Like I did whenever she asked about my schoolwork. My loans. My fucking life.

"I guess so, Mom. He doesn't keep me posted."

"Well, he's really in the shit now with that new article of his. Bone Digger, Gossip Trade, Buzzard Dump. Everyone is blogging about it. Even some of the newspapers have picked it up. Did you see what the *Times* had to say about it this morning? It's all over the editorial page. I wonder sometimes if that man is the philosopher of dirt sandwiches."

I had absolutely no idea what she was talking about, so I humored her. My mother could be very dizzy at times. But in a semi-intellectual way. Kind of like a 1950s poet. Anne Sexton with a spray-on tan. Picture Lucille Ball living on a golf course reciting Kafka in a yellow bikini. That's my mother.

"He did make a mean Cuban medianoche," I said. "And his avocado and sprouts on multi-grain made me look at the world in a whole new way."

She laughed. "Okay, make fun of your old mom. Nothing new there. Kent rolls his eyes at almost everything that comes out of my mouth these days."

"Trouble in paradise?" I asked.

Inside my head, I begged Kali and all the other powerful goddesses to please, *please* let her say, *No trouble, I so love that man.* Because I just did not want to deal with a Mom crisis. Not now, not when I'd finally found a way to make some good money and get at least one part of my pathetic life back on track.

She sniffed. "Oh, no, honey. Nothing of the sort. I so love that man. Ours is a full star ahead kind of love."

Okay. Huh? But things were still good, it seemed.

Relief flooded through me, chasing through my bullet train bloodstream the four cups of high-dose caffeine I'd inhaled upon arising. Last thing I needed now was a visit from a mother in man trouble. I loved my mom, and we were close. But I did not want to kick Ginger off the couch so my mother could lie there in a morose heap, nursing a broken heart. Been there, done that. Over and over.

Behind me, the front door to my building opened. I glanced over my shoulder, then scooted my butt over to one side of the crumbling cement staircase.

"Buck's here, Mom. I gotta go. You home later this afternoon?"

She giggled. "While the cat's away, the girl *can* go feral, you know." She blew a kiss, signed off with sex advice left over from the Kennedy era. "Don't do anything I wouldn't do."

I laughed, but the comment made me stop and think. Would Mrs. Della Flanagan O'Grady Grimwold suck dick and take advantage of rich men in order to make the rent?

Of course she would. And had. Probably still did. When she was my age, she already had me to support. With no high school diploma and tough times in scrubby Florida, my mom surely had fallen to her knees in order to keep a roof over our heads. And what about right now? Was her life really any different? Maybe not. Maybe she loved Kent. But could be she just loved what he did for her. The life he provided her with.

I tucked my phone in a back pocket of my denim shorts. Buck sat down beside me, his bare thigh nestling in, thick and muscled, hairy and warm against mine.

"Whaddup? You girls do what you needed to do last night?"

I nodded. "Oh, yeah. And despite a bunch of tricky snags, we did real good. Your cut of the cash, which we are not sharing with Cedrick7Z since this part of the take needs no fencing, is upstairs. Almost three hundred bucks, and you didn't even have to turn on the oven."

Buck grunted. "Not bad. Not great, but hey, pot peddlers do not complain about extra income."

I could feel his eyes on me so I looked over at him. His five o'clock shadow had turned into a ten a.m. stubble. Sexy. We stared at one another.

"You sure you don't need to pass it through the pimp before you cut me in? I'm not wanting to rile that man. You know what they say about that dude's temper."

Yeah, I'd heard the stories. One girl had gone missing, another walked with a limp. Jerry had warned me. But I wasn't sure I believed the rumors. I couldn't see Cedrick7Z getting his hands dirty. He prided himself on his rapper-style cool. I saw him as a ladies man, kind of a dandy. It was true he had a harshness, a mean streak that showed when the curses came streaming out. So I didn't want him to tear me a new one for something I'd done wrong. But that was all I'd ever witnessed him use. His nasty mouth.

Besides, I was freelance now. Not one of his stable of whores. I had my own stable. And my crew? We were not whores. We were artists. Seduction artists. Rip-off artistes. Robyn Hoodies, women of the street, making us a movement that would right some wrongs in the big city. And funnel some money from the undeserving to the needy.

A girl can always pretend to be a hero, right?

"You get anything else off the mark last night?"

I told him the quick version. Then I took the newly spit-shined Rolex out of my pocket for a minute, let him hold it in his palms and model it on his wrist. It looked damn good on him. The diamond chips were set off beautifully by his coffee and cream skin.

Buck oohed and ahhed. "Sweet." We smiled at one another and he handed it back to me.

"What do you think it's worth?" I asked, tucking the watch back in my front pocket.

"On the street? No idea." Buck shifted his pretty butt and stretched out beside me on the stairs. I could smell his hickory aroma. I wanted to lick his big brown forearm, see if it tasted as smoky as he smelled. I wasn't sure why I bothered to resist him. Was I that afraid I would fall for the man? And what would be so bad about that?

Everything. He had no future. No career. No money. He was an ex-con, a small time drug dealer, a bigger loser than I was. He had a zillion women, all much more beautiful than I could ever pretend to be. He'd never love me, and he'd eventually dump me. Then our friendship would be ruined. I liked our friendship.

"Ginger's still sleeping," I said. "If you want, you can go wake her up. The cash is on the kitchen table. I'm going to Blackbird for breakfast, so you two will have some alone time."

I stood up, avoiding his eyes. He didn't say anything until I caved and looked down at him.

Buck was smiling, but his black eyes were hard, unreadable. "You changing the rule on fraternizing? Why's that, all of a sudden?"

I didn't answer. I walked down the steps, speaking quickly over my shoulder. "Coffee's on. Help yourself. Help yourself to anything you want up there. Be back in an hour."

He grunted and swore under his breath. When I reached the sidewalk, he called out, "You don't know what you want, do you, Shea?"

"Heaven," I called back to him. "Heaven Scent."

My stomach was growling. I walked at a brisk pace up Centre Street to my favorite café, hoping the small restaurant wasn't crowded. I wanted a generous wedge of spinach cheddar quiche, and I wanted it *now*.

****

The Blackbird was delightfully quiet. A few singles sipping cappuccinos from oversize crockery cups in pastel colors. An elderly couple sharing a chocolate croissant at one of two small tables by the front window. Here and there, the ever-present young moms with baby strollers, haggard-looking women with big circles under their eyes. These women jumped up and down, tending to their charges, sucking down the caffeine required to run on empty both night and day. For no pay.

After I ordered a slice of quiche and a shot of

Mickey J. Corrigan

espresso, I bought a copy of the *Times* from the woman behind the counter. I needed to see what my mother had been blathering about. Was there really an op-ed mentioning Antoine's work? Or a reference to something new Tell All had revealed? I hadn't looked at the website for a week or two. Maybe they'd broken a new story on Prince Harry's binge drinking. Or Peter Thiel's secret funding of an underground libertarian gay astronaut about to announce his presidential candidacy or something.

I wished I admired my ex-boyfriend's journalism skills and his notoriety in that regard, but I didn't. He really believed his work made a difference to people. In my mind, the scuttlebutt he worked so hard to uncover was little more than distraction. And weren't we all distracted enough?

I skimmed a story on page one, a weird piece about some kind of Internet bazaar selling all sorts of illegal drugs using an eBay retail format. Buyers and sellers stayed out of legal trouble by downloading free anonymity software. The site's founder was a mystery man who lived in an undisclosed location, surrounded by bodyguards, in hiding from the U.S. government. Poor guy. Wouldn't he rather have a life than a six billion dollar evaluation—and no life?

But the idea itself was brilliant. All you can eat smorgasbord of multi-grade marijuana, coke, crack, LSD, meth, heroin, and ecstasy. Any prohibited mind-altering substance you desire, with only a quick tap on your keyboard, all of it delivered to you in unmarked packaging via the U.S. Postal Service. What suburban housewife, master of the universe, or cockeyed teen wouldn't go for this pain-free method to score—or sell?

116

I'd have to warn Buck, if he didn't already know about the up and coming competition. These sites could put a lot of boots-on-the-ground retailers out of business. In fact, if Amazon versus the brick and mortar bookstores was any indication of the clout of the economic model, it *would* put Buck et al out of business. And soon.

When the steaming slice of quiche arrived, I thanked the multi-pierced, multi-tatted waitress and dug in. Yummy. I scarfed the eggy delight in a flash. The crust was whole-wheat perfection. I had a tiny mouth orgasm, then licked my fork. Wow.

Feeling lazy and still tired from our long night on call, I lingered over my double-shot of potent coffee, skimming articles. Shootings, pederasty, Ponzi schemes, war. The world had already gone to hell in a bread basket. I flipped through the paper to the op-ed page.

Muthafuckahs! Antoine! There he was, featured prominently in an opinion piece above the fold. Tell All had begun to rustle some high-powered feathers Down Under. Due to increasing threats, my ex had gone rogue with materials he'd received from a whistleblower who worked for an Australian diplomat.

Didn't sound like much of a big whoop, but somehow it was high-grade news. I read and reread the essay, a scathing piece from a professor of political science at Harvard Law. Stuffy snob made his point the way the intellectual elite usually do, with no room for reasonable discussion. The Australians were our allies. We didn't expose their dirt. They didn't go messing around in ours.

Only, that was a bunch of brainwashing bullshit.

Us and them? Crap. Nobody bought that patriotic pabulum anymore. Tell All, like so many websites, was borderless. There was no *our* side, no *our* country. Just publishers and readers in a WTF, everybody out for themselves, universally global and who gives a damn, buy one get one free world.

I used my phone to try to jump on the Internet. To cruise around and determine what all the fuss regarding my ex-boyfriend was actually about. But the Internet was down. Maybe Blackbird's cable bill hadn't been paid in a while. Feeling sorry for the counter woman, a flaky pastry in her late teens, and the pixie lesbian waitress with her oversized nose ring, I left a ten under my plate. For once, I could do what I'd always longed to do, leave a generous tip for my underpaid servers.

On the hurried walk back to my place, I was sweating like a roofer in July and talking to myself. If Antoine was in hiding, maybe he hadn't lost interest in me. Maybe he wanted nothing more than to rush back to my welcome embrace, to the soft nest I'd kept clean for his return. Stripped, yes, but definitely cleaner than when he'd left it.

But when I imagined the scene of our reunion, it took place in *my* apartment. Antoine's personal stuff was gone, replaced by my minimalist discomfort. If I visualized it honestly, I could see used coffee cups piled in the clogged—again—sink, the awkward maroon divan strewn with Ginger's clothes, and Buck.

Buck?

Buck. Naked on the divan, his head between Ginger's knees.

I shook myself to dislodge the image from my overcaffeinated brain. I stopped my headlong rush home to remind myself it had only been twenty-five minutes. If I walked in now, I might walk in on Buck and Ginger. I sped up. Seeing them together, well, that might help me stop thinking about the man myself.

Might.

I slowed down again. The day was warming, the sky white blue with only a mouthful of already been chewed clouds. Cars breezed past, hip hop music blaring. What I needed to do was take my time, give the two lovebirds a chance. It would be a mistake for me to go voyeuristic. Hadn't Skipper just told us what a huge turn off that was? Imagine walking in on the man you craved, getting it on with one of your closest friends.

Craved? I slapped myself upside my crazy head. What *was* I thinking? My mind was recreating Buck into some kind of big brown dessert. Like a giant Dove bar.

The onslaught of uninvited thoughts confused and disturbed me. I blamed Della and her bad mother advice.

To run down the clock while I got hold of my runaway imagination, I collapsed on a metal bench in a bus stop cubicle and opened up the newspaper again. Thirty minutes in the shade of the plastic-walled booth ought to do it. I'd sit here, catch up on world news. Knowing the notoriously sparse weekend transit system, I would not be disturbed by any approaching busses.

There was a time for distractions, and this was one of those times.

Only when I was fairly sure the coast was clear at my apartment did I stand up, drop the paper in the overflowing trash can, and take myself on home.

Chapter Eleven

My apartment was silent, the couch neat, the sink sparkling, coffee cups drying on the rubber rack. A note from Ginger next to Mr. Coffee said she'd taken her cut and gone home to Nahant. No mention of Buck. When I counted the remaining cash, his share was still there.

I was surprised by how happy this made me.

Tired but not sleepy enough to lie down for a nap, I spent the rest of the afternoon on my computer, reading articles by and about Tell All. My mother had been right. Antoine and Tell All had gotten themselves into a public mess.

From what I could determine, Antoine was going to find it difficult to leave Australia anytime soon. I hadn't thought the Ozzies were such hard asses. With only around twenty-two million of them spread out over an entire continent, you'd think they'd have room for diverse opinions. A bunch of beer drinking footballers, these folks were only a few generations removed from the British and Irish prisoners who had populated the land as an early form of practical justice. One would think they'd be down with publicly trash-talking their politicians. Not so, as Mary-Ann would say. They held dear their Down Under dirt, played for keeps, and got even with outsiders who blew a cover they didn't want blown.

Antoine was in the shit.

When I turned off my laptop, my head was buzzing. Wow. What did the situation mean for me? Maybe Antoine hadn't been in touch all these months because he *couldn't* contact me. Maybe he'd been imprisoned, redacted, temporarily or even permanently silenced.

I stood up and paced the living room. I needed to stop catastrophizing. I was being ridiculous. The Australians wouldn't seize an American journalist just for revealing the sexual orientation of a high-ranking government official. Would they? Australia wasn't Saudi Arabia. It wasn't Iran. No balls would be chopped off. Would they?

After working myself into a terrible state of giddy anxiety, I took a long walk in the late afternoon sunshine. Hiking through the arboretum and around the pond calmed me. The trees were in bloom, families of Mallard ducks glided together across the still water. All was fine in my little world.

I returned with an adjusted attitude. All was as it should be. A cool shower and a big glass of red wine kept me from reverting to high angst again. I would keep my mind on my own business, not Antoine's.

Dressing for my meeting with my handler was another welcome distraction. Electric pink mini-dress cut up to there, black fishnet stockings, ankle-high disco boots. Bling galore, including the hot Rolex, flashing its worth where nobody would notice it among all the bangles and beaded bracelets.

Looking good, Heaven Scent.

On my way out the door, I decided to drop in on Buck. Maybe I was being flirtatious, popping in on him while dressed in my hooker duds. Maybe not. He'd seen me in worse outfits. He'd put up with me in less.

I counted out Buck's share of the cash, grabbed my gold-fringed clutch, and hustled downstairs.

The earthy reek of pot filled the first floor hallway. The Aggrovators were hard at it on the other side of the building manager's door. Buck needed to diversify. Even if the reggae and the homegrown aroma were all part of his business brand, the scene was getting old. He'd need to compete with the crisp new Internet model for drug sales. Changes were a-coming. Buck would have to do what it took to stay relevant.

I knocked on the door. "Lemme in, Mr. B. I got somethin' sweet for you." My voice was breathy. Heaven Scent was here.

Buck answered right away, as if he had been standing there, waiting for me on the other side of the door. "Hey, girl." He appraised me in a single, sweeping, lingering glance. "On your way to see the entertainer?"

I twirled around for him, swung my ass in a hot little circle. "What d'you think? Do I look the part?"

Buck laughed. "Oh yeah. I'm all cranked up, and we're just friends."

"Aww. You say the cutest things." I handed him his money. "What're you baking in there? Got any crumbs?"

He stuffed the money in the back pocket of his cargo shorts, shutting the apartment door behind him. "Let me walk you out. You're driving, I take it? Wouldn't want you to get on the bus in that getup."

We were in the lobby when I remembered. The Mini still needed a new battery.

"Shit," I said. "I forgot my car's not operational." I

hated riding the T with my cleavage showing. And I didn't want to get on the bus in my fuck-me outfit.

"Lemme give you a lift," Buck said. "I'm just hanging out tonight. No customers."

How nice. "Wow, really?"

"Sure. Let's go. I'm parked right out front."

He even held the door for me while I climbed into the passenger seat of his beat-down Honda Civic. I caught him peeking while I wiggled around, trying to straighten out my skirt.

"Like those fluorescent panties, Heaven," he said before he closed my door for me.

I had to laugh.

While we drove into town, I told him what I'd learned about Antoine's predicament. Buck didn't do any business with Antoine, who'd done his weed buying elsewhere. But he'd heard me talk about my boyfriend a lot, back when he *was* my boyfriend, and he'd put up with all my bellyaching about my ex once he'd gone missing. Buck had known Antoine longer than I had from years of being his building manager.

After I summarized my findings, I asked Buck, "Do you think something horrible has happened to Antoine? Think he's in the outback somewhere, a political prisoner?"

Buck glanced at me and smiled. We'd stopped for a light a few blocks shy of the John Hancock Jazz Bar. "Hope so," he said with a wink. "Hope they Wikileak the guy, and he's stuck in some foreign embassy for years."

"What do you care?" I shifted in my seat to stare at him. Was he kidding? "I know you guys were never friends, but did something happen between you two?"

"Let's just say I don't like the man's style. Don't like what he stands for. Don't like how he treats his woman."

A hot blush crept up my neck to my face. "You're a sweet guy, Mr. B." I leaned over to kiss him on one stubbled cheek. "You can drop me here," I added as we pulled up to the jazz bar entrance.

But Buck kept going. He drove past the bar, took a left into a public parking garage, and went all the way up to the roof level. After parking in a space in the near empty lot, he turned off the engine. Then, before I could say anything, he swept me into his arms.

His lips were full, warm, and tasted like Poptarts. He smelled more like grapes than smoke. I kissed him back, eyes closed, mind full of feeling. Parts of me tingled, reassuring me my libido had not been destroyed by my brief but intense hooking career.

We kissed for a while, exploring one another with our fingers and tongues. Yum, was all I could think. My new mantra—yummmmmmm.

Using all the willpower I could muster, I pulled away. "Can we continue this after my meeting? I feel like we've just gotten started on something."

Buck swept a loose strand of hair off my face, tucking it behind my ear. I licked his palm, his index finger, his thumb. Yum fucking yum.

"Now that you've rescinded the crew rules," he said after another round of passionate kisses, "I thought I'd take advantage of the opportunity to express my feelings. Ginger's been pestering me for days now to tell you how I feel."

I looked into his face, his beautiful face. Buck grinned and cocked his head. His eyes were bright, joyful. "Ginger seems to think you're into me as well."

I hadn't confided in her about my feelings for Buck. I hadn't even confided in myself. Was I that easy for others to read? Guess so. Because the truth was, I'd always been into Buck. Even when Antoine and I were together, I'd had a hankering for the man with the gorgeous Rastafarian locks. What Jamaica Plain female didn't? He was eye candy, and a good guy to boot.

Speaking of boots, mine were pooling with sweat. Leather gear is great for picking up johns, but lousy for make out sessions in summer weather.

I popped open my door. "I *am* into you, Bucko. And I want more of what we started here. So, see you back at the apartment? I mean, can I drop by when I'm done with Cedrick7Z?"

He reached over to touch my lips with one oversize thumb. Mary-Ann would be predicting his dick size based on those big thumbs. I didn't need to guesstimate. I could tell by the bulge in his cargo shorts that he was he-man-sized all over. I fanned my hot face with one hand.

"I can wait for you here, if you like."

Such a gentleman. I could get used to this kind of guy.

"I like. I like very much." I blew a kiss and wriggled out of the seat, flashing my lacy butt on the way. I walked around the car to his window and leaned in for another kiss. "Be back fast as I can."

"I'll be here," Buck put a roach to his lips and flipped his CD player on. The Maytals.

"Remind me to tell you about another article I read today, about online drug sales," I told him before I rushed off to my meeting.

I didn't hurry too much, though. I walked as Marilyn Monroe-ishly as I could to the top floor exit door. Once I was out of Buck's sight, that's when I stopped swishing my ass and started hustling it. Careful not to trip on my four-inch heels, I jogged down the cement stairs, out of the garage and onto the city street.

****

Cedrick7Z ordered me a blue martini after I showed him the Rolex. "Slide that thang over here, honeypot, and let me get you a drink."

Hoping he meant the watch, I took it off my wrist and handed it to him. He set it on the table between us for a moment while he signaled the waiter. It sure was a beauty. My heart flirted with my chest, wildly happy with the way my night was going.

Cedrick7Z moved the watch down to the leatherette banquette beside him. "You come in here with any take, we keep that subtle. 'Kay, babe?"

I nodded. Subtle. Like his chocolate velour dinner jacket and blood-red bowtie? My former handler was quite the caricature of a sex industry hotshot. I had to hand it to him, he looked the part even more than I did.

"Good stuff, puss," he said, looking up from the watch. "Good shit. What else you got for me?"

"This is it, just the Rolex. We had some complications," I explained with a shrug.

Cedrick7Z frowned so hard his creases looked carved. He dropped the watch into a pocket in his jacket, then waited while the waiter set down my drink and retreated. When I reached for the glass, however, my former handler snatched it away. He held it to his fat lips, sipping my martini, luxuriating in my drink.

"I thought—"

"You ready to suck some dirty dick tonight, pussycake? Cuz this one fine piece a bling don't make a take. Make a half a pull, mebbe. They melt that down, yank out all the chips, you and me get a couple a martinis out of it. Possibly more, not much more."

"*What?* That's ridiculous, Ced. I looked it up online. The watch sells for thirty grand new."

"We not sellin' it new. We fencin' it used. And hot. We get what we can get, understand?"

Was he fucking with me? I shook my head. WTF? That watch would be worth thousands if we sold it on eBay.

Then it dawned on me. Fifty percent of whatever he pretended he got, whatever he wanted to give me, that's what I would take home to my crew. I should have known, the dirty fuckboy. I watched him sip the cool blue drink, his gaze like an iguana's, slow-moving and cold.

Bile broiled in its own juices, then burbled on its way to my throat. I felt like strangling the man with his stupid looking red tie. So he was going to play it this way. Lie about value, then keep most of the profits, give me a shitty little kickback cut? Not like I could report him to anyone, sue for lost income.

I must have been giving him the evil eye because he grabbed my hand with one cold black glove and squeezed. Hard.

Ouch.

"You don't know nuthin' about it, bitch. So don't tell me what you don't know."

I nodded, trying to appear sincere, until he let go of my crushed hand. The bones in my knuckles throbbed. Maybe those rumors about Cedrick7Z were more than that. Because my hand hurt like hell. The man had actually hurt me.

He drank most of the rest of my martini, watching me the whole time for a reaction. Then he set the glass back on the linen tablecloth in front of him. "You get me a big muthafuckin' haul, maybe I let you rebrand. 'Til then, you still my girl." He lifted his chin, as if to say, *scram, go suck dick.*

My heart lurched around in the bile lake that had formed in the back of my throat. No way I was hooking. Not tonight, not ever. I'd rather hand over my cash from the night before, lie, tell him I'd earned it for him with some johns.

Time for me to go. I smiled at my former handler, as if we were on the same page of a trashy book. When I stood up, I tottered for a moment, unstable on my four-inch heels.

He gave me a onceover, then beckoned with a crook of his index finger. When I leaned down, hoping he wouldn't grab hold of my neck and crush some of those delicate bones, he whispered in my ear. His breath smelled like my martini. "Got a tip for you and your crew. Basketball team in from out of town. Tomorrow night, they be at the Avalon on Lansdowne."

I stood up again. Cedrick7Z glanced furtively around the soft-lit barroom, then up at me. His raccoon eyes burned, warning me not to fuck it up, not to fuck with him.

He continued in a low voice. "The Springfield Riflemen. And baby, these guys are players, they carry heavy. Like to flash that gold and party hardy. Guns, jewelry, cash, all back at the hotel. The Ritz. All I'm gonna speak on the matter."

What could I say? "I'll get you your money, Ced. You know I will."

"I don't know nuthin' 'til it in my own fist." He held up both gloved hands, squeezed them together in a mockery of his earlier death clasp on my knuckles. Then he gave me the fist pump and mocked me a little more with a black leathered, queenish wave of dismissal.

So much for partnering with a pimp. Shit.

I hurried back to the parking garage where Buck was waiting for me.

Chapter Twelve

While I was telling Buck what Cedrick7Z had said to me in our meeting, he drove slowly up Huntington, listening carefully. He shook his head a few times and, at one point, let out a long low whistle.

By the time I finished my rant, we were passing the Northeastern campus. The urban sprawl of bland institutional buildings seemed to be mocking me. I felt like a fool. Whatever made me think I could just jump into the grift? Why kid myself I could play the seduce and rob game and actually earn? I wasn't even enjoying beginner's luck. And I was making bad decisions. Working with Cedrick7Z? Stupid. And holding back part of the take from that hardass pimp? Ludicrous.

"I'll have to pay him all the cash I earned off the guy from the other night. Unless I want to go traipsing around the Internet tonight, looking for sick twists to suck on." I cracked my window. My feet were sweating under the tight leather of the boots. Certainly not appropriate for summer weather wear and terrible for running in. As usual, I'd gone for style over comfort. Would I ever learn? "But he gave me a good tip for tomorrow night. So there's that."

Buck placed a hand on my thigh, reassuring me he was on my side. Even though I must have been sounding dumb and dumber. "Another con, you mean? And you're going to try to pull it off?"

"I have no choice. I owe Cedrick7Z. It's like I'm indentured. White slavery." I laughed, a mirthless sound. "Why oh why do I always get myself into these fucked up messes?"

"Simple. Because you are creative, but poor. So that's what happens. To people like us." Buck stopped at a red light on Huntington, turned to look at me. He smiled, lifted my sore hand to his lips and kissed it gently. "But maybe there's a safer way for you to get out of debt."

I pulled my hand away. "Don't you think I would've done it already if a better way existed? Believe me, I did not become a hooker for the fun of it. And now, a goddam thief? Not my first choice of careers."

The light changed and we cruised to the next one.

"Don't get mad, Shea. You know I'm coming from similar experience. I'm just saying, maybe we could alter our job descriptions to something legal. With a change in venue."

Leave Boston? I really didn't want to have to do that. Even though I knew Buck was right. Moving on was always an option.

I rested my small pale hand over his big dark one on the black mesh of my stockinged thigh and blurted, "Let's run away together."

He grinned. "You've had worse ideas."

I couldn't wait to kiss him again.

When he parked in a lucky space right across from our apartment building, I was unbuckled, damp, and ready for him. I knew what I wanted. I wanted to kiss him hard and long. So the second he turned off the car, that's just what I did. I lunged, and he laughed into my mouth as he kissed me back. His lips tasted like smoked chocolate chip cookies, and his tongue was even juicier than the first time we'd lip-locked. Umm umm ummmmm.

When I opened my eyes a few minutes later, dizzy, wet now in all the right places, I spotted a flash of white. Across the street, somebody wearing a white hoodie sat on our front stoop.

"Shit," I said. "I've seen that kid before. A few times. What's he doing here?"

Buck looked dazed, his eyes glazed and sleepy. He wiped his mouth with one hand and stared where I pointed. "Not one of my regular customers. But he doesn't look like much of a threat. Let's see what he has to say for himself."

When we got out of the car, the person in the hoodie stood up. He crossed his arms over his chest, and waited for us to walk to the steps. Then he flipped his hood off to reveal a sweet young face. Kid must have been all of seventeen, with big brown eyes and perfect cocoa skin.

"Sorry to bother you folks. Bunny sent me," he said.

"Bunny? I don't know—"

I shushed Buck with a quick squeeze of his delightful biceps. I couldn't wait to run my mouth over his arms. And the rest of his sculpted musculature. But now I would have to.

"I know Bunny," I said. "An old friend. Want to come inside?"

Bunny was my bedroom nickname for Antoine. Nobody had ever used it except us. And now, for whatever reason, this kid.

"My place or yours?" I asked Buck as we entered the lobby.

"Mine is fine. Unless Bunny's friend here is in law enforcement," he said with a grin.

I shook my head. "Not much chance of that. He still doesn't have his driver's license."

The kid stopped to text someone before he followed us down the hall to the manager's office.

"This better be good," Buck whispered to me as he unlocked the door. "And fast. I have important plans for us this evening. I don't want to have to wait. I've already been waiting for too long."

I reached for his head and pulled it toward me so I could give him a quick kiss on the lips. "Me, too. I don't want to wait any longer, either."

Unfortunately, I would have to. We both would.

Bunny's messenger stood in the doorway to Buck's apartment and sniffed. "Smells good in here," he said with a bright smile. The boy was cute, clean-cut, appealing.

Buck frowned. "Let's get through this, okay, kid? So, what's the deal?"

The kid stopped smiling. "Bunny wants to talk to you," he said to me. "If you're down with that, I'm supposed to call him, hand you the phone. That cool with you?"

I nodded. After all this time, this was how Antoine chose to contact me again? Via a street kid in a hoodie? My life had gone from bad to weird.

The kid talked in a low voice for a moment, then passed me his smart phone. I gave Buck what I hoped was a calm, everything is gonna be fine—and I will make this *damn* quick—look, then turned my back and walked off to stand by the living room window. The streetlights out front cast a buttery sheen over everything they touched. Buck's Honda, the dogwood trees, the cyclone fence around the empty lot across the street. My heart went fluttery, and I suddenly felt breathless. Like I'd been interred.

Heartbeat pittering and pattering, I closed my eyes. "Hello? Bunny?"

"Hi, Sugarbear." Antoine's bedroom name for me. My knees weakened. He sounded far away, distant and weak.

"You okay? Where are you? What the hell is going—"

He cut me off, talking rapidly in a low, strangled voice. I had to strain to hear, so I put a finger in my other ear to block out the sound of Buck's pacing, the popping of bottle caps, the background banter with Antoine's messenger. It was difficult to decipher what my old boyfriend was saying, but I did understand part of his hurried monologue. He was in hiding, the role of espionage journalism in digital politics was under hostile fire from various governments around the world, the website was being threatened, there was more information coming that would unsettle certain powerful people, and therefore he couldn't come home. Not now. Maybe ever.

"Hey," I interrupted. "What does any of this have to do with me?"

My knees were fine now, my heartbeat steady. In fact, I'd quickly grown bored with his monologue, and the call was beginning to annoy me. I'd delayed my romantic rendezvous with Buck long enough. I glanced over my shoulder and gave my man a onceover. He'd removed his T-shirt to reveal that lovely formation of pectorals I so longed to touch. And kiss. And smear myself across. I tried to catch his eye, but he was talking to the kid about something. I caught the word "reggae."

"I just wanted you to know that I didn't leave you, Shea. I wanted us to work out. I mean, I know we had our issues, but we had damn good chemistry. And I cared for you."

I should have said something, like how I loved him, too. But I didn't. Because, because…because fuck him! Fuck him and his work before love attitude. Fuck him and his too late apology. I was done grieving the loss of a man who'd let me down.

So all I felt at that point was irritation. All this time he'd wanted to but couldn't call? And now he tells me? After I spent all those long lonely months feeling like an ugly pile of dirty underwear left at the bottom of a laundry chute? After I debased myself and resorted to Got Hooker dot com? While he was off in cyberspace being a freedom writer, a neo-media superhero or something?

"So, Sugarbear, listen. You can move into my apartment if you want. Use my furniture, drive my car. Okay?"

Been there, done that. I hadn't needed his permission, either.

"Okay, whatever." But my voice caught. Fuck me, I was choked up.

"Please don't cry, baby. I miss you, too. But we have this unbelievable source who's mining some of the most important information about a foreign ambassador ever—"

"Please, stop right there," I said, my voice a sissy sob. "I'm not interested in your undercover blues. And I've lost interest in us. There is no us. There's only you and your damn work. So, go for it. Hope it makes you happy. I promise I'll take good care of your bed. And not fuck more than ten guys a week in it."

Now I was weeping angry tears, my voice a clog of salty phlegm. I doubted Antoine had understood a word of what I'd said. I cleared my throat, then told Antoine exactly what I wanted from him. Spyware.

To my surprise, he agreed at once.

I marched across the room and gave the phone to the kid, who was sharing a skinny joint with Buck. The boy wandered away, talking quietly to Antoine.

Buck handed me his beer. "So Bunny is code for Antoine, I assume."

I gulped some warm Bud.

He passed me the joint. "He coming back?"

I let out a long stream of blue smoke, coughing a little. "Nope."

Buck nodded again. "But you're still hung up on him."

I didn't answer. Was I? My head sure wasn't. But some part of me was—the unthinking, overfeeling, clitorally directed part of me. Why oh why did I always fall for unavailable men?

"Sorry to break up your evening, folks." The kid stood by the front door, his hand on the doorknob.

"Hey, what about the stuff I asked for? Did Bunny tell you what I'm going to need?" I hurried over before he could slip out and disappear into the city night.

The kid was on board. "Yeah, no worries. I'll be back in a few hours with everything, show you how to set it all up. You be here or at your place?"

Without looking at Buck, I said, "I'll be upstairs. In fact, I'm headed there now. I'll leave with you."

So I did. And Buck didn't try to stop me.

Chapter Thirteen

One hour before we were due to meet her in the lobby bar at the Ritz, Mary-Ann called. I'd just stepped out of the shower, and my hair was dripping down my back and all over the floor.

"Not gonna make it tonight, sorry," she said. I could hear babies in the background. One was crying, the other one goo-gooing.

"No sitter?" I tried to scoop my hair into a towel with my free hand.

"I have…something else to do," she said.

That's when I heard the guy's voice in the background. Mary-Ann laughed and said *shh*.

"Is that Kyle?" I already knew what her answer would be. A baby stopped crying. The other one giggled.

"Jaysus, you oughta be a PI. You're too good. Yes, we've been seeing each other. Since that night." She lowered her voice. "He's so into the kids. I fucking love the guy. We're moving in together."

Shit. So that was that, then.

"Cool. He did seem like a nice guy, before we knocked him unconscious." I sighed. Might as well face the facts because they were headed right for me. "So you're off the crew for good. Is that what you're saying, Mary-Ann?"

I hit speakerphone so I could towel dry my hair. I

was happy for her. I really was. But her good fortune reduced the size and reach of my girl gang significantly. I had the feeling Buck would be bailing as well. His feelings had been hurt by my emotional response to Antoine's phone call. Now his hurt feelings were getting in the way of our business. Which was why I'd instituted the no fraternizing rule to begin with. All the fraternizing, it was wrecking my posse!

"Hold on," she said, then, "Can you still hear me?"

Her voice echoed, as if she'd moved to the bathroom. Which she probably had. I couldn't imagine she had much privacy living with her parents, brother, and two small children.

"Heaven, I'm really sorry. But the seduce and steal gig, it just isn't for me. Because what about when the mark turns out to be a sweetheart? Like Kyle? Can't bring myself to rob a man who treats me well in bed. Or on the way to bed. Guess I wasn't much of a team player to begin with. Too into my own feelings. Make all my decisions that way. You guys would've tossed me off the island. Eventually."

She flushed the toilet. Nice camouflage. I wasn't so sure Mary-Ann had been wrong for the job. Women are usually fairly skilled at deception. It may be inborn, an inherited survival skill, a natural trait. Like nurturing. Or shopping.

"Look," I told her. "We're probably gonna get a good haul tonight. I'll still cut you in on the pull. Not a full share, but something."

When I stopped rubbing my scalp with the towel, I caught a sight of my face in the mirror. I looked like shit warmed over. Worry lines creased my freckled forehead, dark circles underlined my eyes. My mouth

turned down at the corners like an upside-down U. I
needed to be kissed, and it showed.

I looked away, hung up the bath towel on its brass-
plated rack. One bath towel, one hand towel, one lousy
face cloth. If they'd been monogrammed, it would've
been with the number one. As in, I live alone. I *am*
alone.

"Wow. You're kidding," Mary-Ann said.

"Over the last couple days, you've been heavily
involved in the planning stages and the crew owes you
something for your efforts. The new spy equipment
we've been practicing on, that shit wasn't easy to learn
how to use, and you spent a lot of time messing around
with it. Plus, my handler still hasn't paid out for the last
gig. And if we hadn't had your truck, that might not
have gone so well."

Not that it went *well*, exactly. But still, we *had*
pulled it off.

I parted my wet hair, combed it off my face.
Someday I would invest in a blow-dryer. Someday I
would do what was comfortable. Then I would be able
to stop asking myself why oh why I always did
everything the hard way.

But not today.

"Appreciate it, Heaven. You're sweet. Your man
comes through on that watch, let me know. You hit it
big tonight and there's extra, sure, swing some my way.
Kyle put a deposit on a three-bedroom with a backyard.
In Canton. Mark's coming with. It's a dream come true,
only muthafuckin' suburbia? I'm moving to the 'burbs,
Heaven. Tell me it's not so. Not so!"

We laughed. I promised to update her on the results
of tonight's gig. The plan was to seduce the Springfield

Riflemen.

"Those guys are all gonna be hung. Dicks like assault rifles," she predicted. "Think about their size sixteen feet."

After we hung up, I took the phone with me into the bedroom. I needed to call the gang, tell them the change in Mary-Ann's status. Lucky I'd washed my hair. Because it looked like I'd be subbing for our missing crew member. I would have to stand in tonight's lineup of sexy seductresses on the prowl for a seven-foot sap. A big tree with sap running, I thought. Tree with a giant woody.

I chose some sexy underwear and wriggled in. Lacy silk was always a turn on. I needed to get pumped. Because before Mary-Ann had signed herself out, I'd expected to wear my cotton panties and coordinate the action from the safety of the Mini. The plan had been to let the other three hook up with one or more willing, blinged out, out-of town ball players. Now I'd have to join in the game.

I perused the contents of my closet and went with my shortest, tightest black dress. Entrepreneurship may have been the new black. But the little black dress? It was as old as I was, yet still a hundred percent now.

Black itself was timeless.

****

In the Ritz lounge, we split up and staked out the soft-lit, high-ceilinged room. One hot girl in the three o'clock, six 'o'clock, and nine o'clock positions. My seat at the circular oak bar allowed me to keep watch for tall heads on the way to or fro. I could see through the entryway perfectly, all the way out to the pink marble lobby. When the players came down from their rooms, they would pass by the lounge on their way to the cab stand. One might come in for a drink before heading off to club through the night. If one did, he would be ours.

That was the plan, anyway.

Highly polished brass seemed to be the theme for the bar décor. Oak and brass and real honest-to-god leather. A faint odor of Cuban cigars blended with the smell of French perfume and Irish whiskey. The place reminded me of a turn of the century gentleman's library. Doddery bald guys in cartoonish glasses huddled together in brown leather booths with shiny brass railings. Spiffy young exec types sipped from cut crystal glasses while eye-fucking their Barbie Does Boston dates. All the Roger Vivier shoes, the Hermès Birkin pocketbooks, the Chanel jackets and Piazza Sempione blouses. The trendy Fendi bags. The ropes of pearls, the Cartier watches, Hugo Boss and way too much Ralph Lauren. The bar patrons put me into a dulled trance with their uniformed luxury. All of it unreachable, held out before me but at arm's length.

An attractive middle-aged woman in a navy blue silk dress with a rather daring V-neck sat beside me at the bar, nursing a Cosmo. Her shoes were Manolo Blahnik, her purse a Louis Vuitton cross body bag. I wondered what her story was. Fired ad exec? Unhappy doctor's wife? Attorney in the middle of a nasty divorce? Her own, perhaps?

She caught me sizing her up and smiled. "This place is not happening tonight," she told me in a confidential tone. "And I have a Mercedes lease payment that is weeks overdue."

I must have looked startled because she patted my

arm. "Don't worry, I won't be any competition for you and your friends. I'm in an entirely different market. You girls are seeking wealthy older men who want to spend a few hours with a delicious young woman. They will pay for you to accompany them upstairs for a few hours. I'm here for the rich boys. Prep school grads with Daddy's charge cards. Young men who tend toward dull, but are smart enough to know they need to learn the hills and dales of the female anatomy." She winked one heavily mascaraed eye.

What could I say to that? I shrugged. "I'm supposed to meet my boyfriend here. But he's late." In case she turned out to be an undercover cop.

She nodded. "Good girl. You'll do all right." She sipped her drink. "Twenty years ago, I sat exactly where you're sitting. I was broke, wearing a skirt I'd bought at Filene's basement. Now I live in Brookline in a lovely condo." She reached over a finely manicured hand to pat my arm. "It's a hell of a life, you need to be able to ride the ups and downs. Do save for your future, darling. Because it becomes more difficult with each passing year."

She slid a twenty across the bar for the bartender and slipped off her barstool. She had to be forty-eight, maybe fifty, but she was still in excellent shape. Nice shiny hair, trim physique. Would I look that good in another two decades? Would I still be selling myself, still conning men to pay my bills? The thought frightened me. I sipped my Perrier carefully.

Nodding once at me, my new mentor walked out of the bar. I watched her enter the lobby, her head held high, her shoulders back. Where were her loved ones, husband, kids, boyfriends, lovers? Where was the career trajectory that brought her a measure of success based on something other than an ability to seduce needy men? She left the hotel and disappeared from view but not from my mind. I knew I wouldn't forget her.

I ordered a second Perrier. Ginger gave me a *what's happening* look, and I shrugged. After that, I sat there waiting, checking my phone for the time a bit too often. And god, the wait was interminable. To amuse myself, I made faces at Ginger and Mary-Ann whenever one or the other looked over. By eleven, I was growing sleepy and ready to abandon my post. I gave the girls the signal, receiving back a flash of the peace sign from two corners of the bar.

Out front, we bivouacked to advance our plan. If Mohammed couldn't get the mountains to come to the bar, then the smash girls would go to the mountains. Or something like that.

Skipper flagged down a cab, and we piled in.

"Avalon, please," I told the cabbie.

He nodded and stared at me in his rearview mirror. He had a full head of linen wrap, and he smelled like cumin. Shit, he could have been taking us to Riyadh.

"It's not what it looks like," I told him. "We're headed to a costume party."

The girls giggled, but I wasn't at all sure why I was lying about our outrageous clothing. I guess I didn't want to offend his culture. If the Australians could get vindictive over a couple of adults electing to cater to orifices less commonly filled, then what would Punjab think of the three of us? I didn't want to insult him, but my legs were bare right up to my panties, which were neon green; Ginger wore an aqua see-through silk blouse that left little to the imagination. And Skipper was decked out in a skin-tight, black and white jumpsuit and a glittery headband. She looked like an athletic version of Catwoman. Girl should have come off as a fashion fool, but she didn't. Just the opposite. She looked hotter than ever.

Our cab driver raised his bushy brows. "Ten minute fare, ten dollar minimum. You could walk. Maybe not in those shoes."

I resented his footwear critique, but he had a point. Plus, I could hardly blame the man for judging our books based on their Playboy covers. "Ten is fine." I went light on the tip.

Thing about living in the U.S. was, it wasn't like where you came from. So fuck it, you just had to adapt.

Lansdowne Street was a mob scene. The post-Red Sox game crowd mixed with college kids fresh from keg parties and the regular rowdy drunks. We sashayed—yes, we did—across the street and straight to the front door of Avalon. Bold in our cheesiness, we went right up to the velvet ropes. Okay, yeah, we did cut to the front of the line, ignoring the murmur of protests from people who had been waiting, steeping in sweat and stale beer, maybe for hours. But the bouncer, a voluminous black man with a shiny dome and an eye for Skipper, let us right in.

Before we entered the nightclub, Skipper turned around and blew a kiss to the folks in line. To my surprise, nobody booed. Instead, a young woman yelled, "You go, girl." A few others chorused their agreement.

Living proof Skipper could get away with almost anything she desired. She just needed to learn that truth about herself.

"Go to the head of the class, baby," some guy yelled as we headed inside.

So we went. Inside the cool, dark club, we stood for a moment to let our eyes adjust. The place was cavernous, loud, and way too dark.

We wandered down a short musty hall that let out on the open space of the dance club. The warehouse-size room pulsed with techno music and the heaving, thrusting crowd. In spite of the sparkling lights thrown off by the spin of decades-old disco balls, it was difficult to see anything beyond the dancing crowd. But after a minute of allowing my night vision to kick in, I spotted the basketball team. Like giraffes in a gator farm, the boys stood above the rest of the animals on the loose on a jacked-up Friday night in Beantown.

I led the way to the least crowded of the four bars and ordered a bottle of sparkling water.

"Fuck that," Skipper said. "Get me a double Smirnoff on the rocks. I need some liquid courage. I like my men built, but those guys are scary big."

Ginger agreed. "If she hadn't pooped out on us, Mary-Ann would be saying how they all have huge dicks. Right? I can hear her saying that right now, in my mind."

"She already predicted that," I told them, and we laughed.

None of us begrudged our former crewmate her romantic happiness. We'd just have to make do with the three of us until I could find a replacement. Without Buck's help. I sucked down my water, burped into my hand, and ordered a shot of Select Silver.

"Make that two," Ginger said.

"Now you two girls are makin' decent sense," Skipper joked. "You wanna fuck with da big boys, you gotta get your mojo on."

I shivered. "I gotta get my slut juices flowing, that's for sure." I was still feeling bad about Antoine and confused about Buck. And I had nobody to confide in. Antoine had sworn me to secrecy for reasons having to do with his own personal security or so he'd claimed. And I didn't want to admit to the girls that I'd broken the crew rules with Buck. "I need to loosen the fuck up."

Skipper laughed, tipped her glass at me, and sucked down her drink. Impressive.

The tequila tasted so damn smooth, I had to order us a second round. And a third. Skipper stuck to her vodka. Soon enough, all three of us were giggly high and ready to approach the marks. Nothing like a few shots of hundred proof to make lassoing a wild animal seem more appealing.

"The tall guy with the Armani suit, he's not so bad," I yelled in Skipper's ear. "Why don't you take him on?"

"The *tall* guy? You got to be kidding me. Which one do you mean? The *tall* guy." She shook her head at me, but she was laughing. "I like the one with the solid gold necktie. That who you mean?"

I didn't know what the man's necktie was made out of, but she'd said she liked him. This was promising. So I said yes, go for it. After all, Skipper would be the crew member most likely to be lured back to the hotel by a celebrity basketball player. Ginger and I might flirt, we could hang around the players and act sexy, but we might not be invited to whore down with these guys.

They had an entourage. Groupies galore. Skipper, on the other hand, would be attended to, she would be wooed, and she would leave with a ballplayer tonight. There was no doubt in my mind about that.

"You girls come with," she said, placing her empty glass on the bar. "Let's ambush these guys. Hit 'em with our rhythm sticks."

"Why not?" Ginger said.

So we did.

****

It was like I was being smothered by twenty sacks of cement. Cement that reeked of Old Spice and Sam Adams amber. I waited for three loud snores before I began to squirm. Finally, I wriggled free of my date.

I gently removed the glasses from my face. It felt like my forehead and cheeks had been stamped with their imprint. And my frigging neck was killing me.

The bedroom was womb dark, so I pulled open the heavy drapes for some street illumination and dug around for my push-up bra. I texted Ginger, then slipped my dress on. I had to search all over the massive hotel suite until I finally found my strappy sandals tossed under a floral arm chair in the living area.

As I headed into the bathroom to slap water on my face, somebody tapped at the door. I rushed over, let her in.

"You hear from Skipper, yet?" I asked in a soft voice while Ginger appraised the situation. Yes, I was dressed, and yes, I appeared unhurt. But why couldn't I meet her eye? Had something unpleasant happened with the brazen ball player? "She still with Denver?" I asked, turning away.

Ginger whispered, "Don't ask. Let's do what we need to do." Then she went over to the king-size bed to check on the mark.

I bent over the pink marble sink and splashed cool water on my flushed cheeks. If I'd been a virgin, I would still be intact. But I wasn't a virgin, and he'd been rough. My body felt tender, everything mildly violated. A familiar feeling, one I had not intended to re-experience.

My life had been on a new track. Then Antoine had re-emerged. And then this. Shit happened. Shit got real again on me. Real ugly, real quick.

I rinsed out my mouth with tepid water and dried my face with a towel about a hundred times fluffier than the one at my apartment. *Ouch.* That crick again. After I soaked a thick face cloth with hot water, I held it to the nape of my neck.

The mark was a famous face, a celeb in the wide weird world of professional sports. But the man was, in my learned opinion, a lowlife bastard. He'd been mean-spirited, a nasty bed partner. I was going to enjoy robbing him blind.

As soon as I came out of the bathroom, we went to work. Ginger gently stripped off the Rolex, the six diamond rings, the tiny diamond studs adorning his ears, his nipples. We left the gold ring on his foreskin. She giggled when she spotted the dick ring, but I didn't laugh. It wasn't funny. Try putting all that in your mouth when someone six-foot-eleven is shoving your head down.

I went through his fat leather wallet. Thick wad of cash, and the key to the hotel safe. I pocketed the bills, mostly hundreds. Then I opened the closet door, and there it was. A walk-in safe in a walk-in closet. My heart sped up and rounded a few corners as I unlocked the thick steel doors.

"Ginger. Come here," I said in sotto voice. She appeared at my side. "We hit the mother lode."

"Holy shit," she whispered. "Who the fuck is this guy? A jeweler?"

"Nope. A jeweler's best customer."

We tucked gold grilles, chains, and rings, plus a handful of loose gems in the collapsible backpacks we both had hidden in our cocktail purses. Guy had a diamond fetish. A set of brilliant-cut single-drop earrings and some antique chandelier earrings? This stuff alone had to be worth a few months of dribbling the NBA ball. What? Did he loan the earrings to his women when they went out on dates? I couldn't see him wearing them himself. He also had a chunky diamond bracelet you'd see in a glass case at Tiffany's or Cartier's. I needed my sunglasses on, the dazzle was so bright.

Underneath the bling on a separate safe shelf sat an impressive pile of cash. More hundreds. This dude did not travel light.

"Should we take everything?" Ginger asked me.

Or maybe she was just talking to herself. She wanted to know what was right. Should we hurt the man as much as possible or show him a little mercy?

I had no mercy for this one. "Strip the fucking safe, and let's get out of here. I don't ever want to see that muthafuckah again."

"I know someone who won't be watching any NBA games this season," Ginger teased.

I didn't respond. I appreciated what she was doing,

trying to lighten the mood. But things were dark inside my head. I felt like a dirty, used up, beaten and scarred old whore horse. And I hated the feeling. How much time did I have on the planet? How much of it was I going to waste feeling like shit about myself?

When we got into the elevator with our overloaded backpacks and pushed the button for the lobby, I finally let out a deep-held breath. I hadn't realized I'd been holding it in. But I guess I'd stopped breathing normally. Probably when my date had sucked down his doctored beer in a single greedy guzzle, then pushed me onto the hotel bed and demanded through diamond studded teeth, "Enough chitchat. Gimme some of that sweet pussy, baby."

I hate men who talk like porn stars.

Sometimes I hate men.

So when Ginger said, "I guess Mr. Point Guard was worth all the irritation he may have caused you," I actually laughed. I laughed and laughed. I laughed until I couldn't breathe. Again.

The elevator continued its slow descent from the top floor. Ginger flipped her bulky pack over one shoulder and seized my upper arm. "Oh, shit. You okay, Heaven?"

I tried to say yes, but I couldn't. I just kept laughing, alternately inhaling big gulps of the poor quality elevator air. Finally, I had to put my head between my knees, I was howling and gasping so hard. Pretty soon, tears were streaming out my eyes.

Ginger let me vent. Then she said, "We're almost to the lobby, sweetie. Can you get it together?"

I managed to stand up straight.

"Doors are opening," she warned. "Chill."

I wiped my face on the back of my hands and got a grip. By the time the brass doors had parted, I was in control. I followed Ginger out of the elevator, down the back stairway, and out the back door to the street.

The night air cooled my sticky skin. I took a huge breath, shaking my head as if to cleanse my mind of all the bad thoughts. When I started to speak, Ginger said, "Shush. Wait."

Skipper pulled up almost immediately in her pale green Volkswagen. I assumed she'd retrieved it from the parking garage where we'd left it at the start of the evening. But where was Denver's loot? In the trunk?

"Going my way, ladies?" She seemed way too chipper. No way she'd hit up the mark tonight. So what had she been doing while I was in a celebrity suite getting mauled by a testosterone monster? "Those packs look mighty heavy," she cooed with a grin.

I dumped myself into the backseat and tried to control my surging emotions. Skipper and I stared at one another in the rearview mirror.

"Don't ask," she said.

So I didn't. I sat there with two backpacks stuffed with cash, jewelry, and other extravagant loot, and I tried not to cry.

Chapter Fourteen

We were on Centre Street a few blocks from my house when Skipper cleared her throat. "I guess I'm just not cut out for this. I hate to admit to being a total pussy, but I'm tendering my resignation."

We stared at one another in the mirror again. My eyes filled up with the tears I'd been fighting so hard to hold back.

"Hey, girl, sorry to poop out on you," she told me. "But I can't deal with sexually aggressive males. Even for a payoff like the one it looks like we got tonight." She eyed the packs in the mirror, then flicked on her blinker to turn down my street. "I don't want to hate men. All this time spent in bars looking for guys, wearing sexy costumes, and hanging around the pickup scene, pulling one night stands with creeps I don't even like? It's messing with my head."

I sniffled. "Yeah. S'okay. I had a bad time of it myself tonight. I'm about ready to punch out my own time card."

Ginger turned around in the passenger seat to pat my knee. "Let's reassess here," she said. "With Mary-Ann off to the greener pastures and A-rated schools of suburbia, the seduce and rob gang is falling apart anyway. We scored big tonight. Real, real big. Enough could be enough, right? We're all woman enough to know when it's time to say we done good, let's move on. Right, girls?"

She withdrew her hand to run it through her curls, then she and Skipper exchanged smiles.

Jeez, what was with those two? Ginger seemed way more perky than the situation warranted. I wasn't sure why. Unless she'd wanted to quit, too, and now she wouldn't have to lose face. Maybe she was glad she'd never had to do more than lug away the haul in a rucksack.

Stewing silently, I watched the two of them for a minute. There was something going on between them, something intimate. Maybe they'd been planning their defection for a while now. Maybe they'd decided how to jump ship while I was up in the hotel room getting molested by the jackal with the diamond canines.

I started to get a little hot under my nonexistent collar. "What were you two up to while I was on my back in the penthouse suite, waiting for my two hundred and seventy pound date to pass out on top of me?"

My voice sounded pissy, but I didn't care.

"Chill, Heaven," Ginger said. "It's not like that."

Skipper scouted for spaces, saw none, continued on to circle the block. "We can talk more once we go up to your apartment, but let me just say, we saw everything going on with you and that animal. Until you took off the spy glasses, we could see everything he did. And it was horrendous to watch. Absolutely horrendous. The man should go to jail for rape. Or attempted rape."

"We cheered when he conked out," Ginger added. "Lucky the idiot sucked all that E down so quickly. Because we were actually discussing coming up to the joint with a hotel manager and getting you out of there."

"But we figured you'd get really mad," Skipper said. "And since you're the one who actually has some hooker experience, we figured you knew what you were doing."

Skipper and Ginger looked at one another, the two of them in total agreement. They were the good guys. They'd wanted to rescue poor little badass me.

How fucking sweet.

I played with the plastic zipper on one of the backpacks. *Did* I know what I was doing with the john? Did I know what I was doing with my frigging *life*? No and no. But would I have been angry if they'd stormed in with the night manager? Probably. After licking that trick's smeggy jewels, I needed to get paid. And after all he'd put me through, I wanted the man's whole stash. I felt I deserved one helluva payoff.

I'd done it. Seduced and robbed, and my vagina still as pure as the day had been fucked up. So why did I feel like my tender skin was smudged with sticky paw prints? Indeliblc marks that would never come off? Made me wonder whether any amount of take was worth feeling this nasty.

Skipper wedged her car into a tight spot a block from my apartment, and the three of us piled out. She didn't pop the trunk, so that confirmed it. She had not scored.

Without any discussion, I let the two of them carry the backpacks. My body was tired, my back muscles sore. And my neck hurt like mad. I needed a long hot bath. And a new career.

We trooped silently upstairs and down the hall to my apartment. I wanted to get a few things settled before I got out the scented candles, soft music, and red wine. I needed to ask a few questions before I cleaned off the bad sex stench in a hot bath overflowing with sweet-scented bubbles.

I flipped on the lights, and we gathered in the living room. The girls opened the backpacks and spread the loot on the floor. Still not speaking, the three of us sat down on the couch together. We stared at the cash, the gold bling, the loose gems, a handful of silver coins I hadn't noticed before. Diamonds of various sizes, plus what looked like sapphires, sardonyx, and black onyx. Was that ivory?

We were silent for a few minutes. Then somebody sighed, and one of us started to make weird noises. Soon enough, we were all cooing at the take. Awwing like moms do while observing the wonderment of their newborn babies.

What was happening to us? Were we experiencing something spiritual? Were we being born again? Was that it? Were the possibilities of new lives opening up before our very eyes?

"Wow." Ginger sighed, ending our reverent meditation over the night's incredible haul. "Wow fucking wow."

"The cash alone is a freaking mindblow," Skipper said in a very soft voice. "We hit the *über* jackpot. Or *you* did, Heaven." She slid a silky smooth arm around my shoulder. "You had the big creep sized up instantly. And you came on to him like a heat-seeking missile. Man never knew what hit him. You had him by the balls before he could even buy you a second drink."

I shrugged, but it was nice of her to compliment me. I don't know how I knew he had tons of bling back in his hotel room. The diamonds in his incisors, though, had served as a pretty good hint.

"So what happened to his teammate, the one you were talking to, Skip? Denver really seemed to like you. Did you dump him or what?"

Skipper and Ginger exchanged glances. If I'd been paranoid, I might have worried about their plans for the loot. But I knew my posse. They weren't going to screw me out of my share. Something else, however, was up with them.

"He's sweet. Denver is a really nice guy. Unlike your date, mine was not into jumping my bones. Warm but cool, if you catch me. He invited me back to the hotel, but not up to his room. We hung out in the bar for an hour or so. Sat in a booth, drank tea, chatted. He loves playing ball, but the man has other plans for his future. He wants to go to medical school. Be a pediatrician."

WTF? I'm upstairs getting my hair pulled, and she's talking educational plans with Mr. Nice? I lifted her arm from my shoulder and stood up. "So, did you go up to his room?"

Skipper shrugged. "He didn't invite me. He asked for my phone number, asked if I wanted tickets to the charity game they're in town for. They play on Sunday. Man shook my hand out on the steps before he went back inside and headed for the elevators." She glanced at Ginger. "So what could I do? I texted Ginger, and she met me out front. We went back to the car and waited for you, watched what was going down with you. Saw the whole thing on the tablet you got from that kid you know."

They thought Freeman Dorff was my source for the

new high-tech gadgetry we'd used for tonight's heist. I couldn't tell them about Antoine.

Skipper shivered. "Your guy was a scary prick. Real cold sonuvabitch. You did so well with that shit, Heaven. I'm in total awe." She sighed. "But Denver? No way I could rip that man off. He's a really great guy."

I couldn't stand it. I turned on her. "Are you shitting me? What about his stupid gold tie? I thought we'd agreed he was nothing but a flamboyant asshole just asking to get stripped of his bling?"

"That's what we thought," Skipper said. "But sometimes we're just plain wrong. Sometimes we jump to the wrong conclusions about men, don't we?" She sounded sad. I had no idea why.

"The gold tie was a joke," Ginger cut in. "He wore it on a dare. It's your guy's necktie. He bet Denver he wouldn't wear it out for the night. Said he was a pussy if he wouldn't wear the thing to Avalon."

"How do you even know this?" I asked Ginger, who was fiddling with her curls. Maybe I was making her nervous. Steam might have been coming out of my ears. "Weren't you busy talking to his freaking teammate with the accent, the guy from the islands?"

"Juan's the one who told me about the bet," Ginger said. "And he commented on how unusual it was for Denver to even be out with them. That guy is super straight. Rarely drinks, never parties."

Fuck me. So Skipper is talking grad school with the Mormon doctor and I'm getting man-handled by the two-ton misogynist? I went straight to the kitchen for the open bottle of Two Buck Chuck I had in the fridge. I was trying not to freak out, but I felt fucked over in every way.

"We knew you'd be upset. Especially the way that guy was treating you tonight," Ginger said. "So we talked it over. And we think you should take half the score. We'll split the other half, divide it up three ways with Mary-Ann. Okay?"

I got a wine glass out of the kitchen cabinet and poured myself some lousy red. My hands were shaking. I needed to relax. Talking about business wasn't going to help me do that.

"I'm taking a bath. You two can crash in my bedroom. I'll sleep on the couch. We can straighten this out tomorrow."

I looked at the digital clock on the stove. Three-thirty. Soon enough, the robins and blue jays would be making gleeful spring morning noises outside my window. Making me feel even more depressed. Why oh why hadn't I been born a bird?

"I mean, we'll talk later on today. After I get some sleep. After I stop hating your guts."

Skipper and Ginger exchanged meaningful glances again.

Fuck them. I stomped into the bathroom and shut the door. Hard.

****

I didn't fall asleep until after the sun came up. The girls weren't sleeping either. After my luxurious bath and rough all-over scrub with my toughest loofah, while I paced the living room drinking more bad wine, I couldn't help it. I overheard them. Whispering, giggling, goofing around like a couple of teenagers. It made me so mad I polished off the rest of the bottle. Finally, with the zesty song birds reminding me of my lowly branch on the tree of life, I passed out.

When I stumbled over to the kitchen, it was almost noon. What was left of my crew had left a scrawled message by the full coffee pot. *At Blackbird, come join us.* My heart jumped a hurdle, and I dashed back to the living room.

My fears were ridiculous. The loot was fine. All the cash and carry had been carefully returned to the backpacks, which were sitting on the floor by the entertainment center.

Sipping the first in what would be a long line of full cups of extra-strong coffee, I decided my number one duty of the day would be to secure a safe place to hide the take. Fortunately, I knew who I might enlist to help me.

The sleepless night had allowed me the time I needed to reevaluate my life. And I had come to some conclusions. Drunken conclusions but conclusions nevertheless. One was, there was nothing wrong with me. In fact, I knew exactly who I was and what I wanted. And it was high fucking time I went for it.

****

When I knocked on his door, my heart stuttered like a madman. But he answered instantly and pulled me inside. His lips were as soft and sweet as I remembered. I tasted mustard, possibly pastrami on rye. I wanted to eat his tongue and go from there.

I had business to attend to first. After the best makeup kiss of my life, I pulled away gently and told Buck what had happened, what was going to happen, and what I would need from him. He listened carefully, running one tender hand through my hair, petting me softly. Occasionally he nodded, considering, weighing my words.

Finally, he kissed the top of my head. "I like the way you're thinking. Good. Let's do it."

So we did.

But we had something to attend to first. A more pressing priority.

I grabbed him around the neck and pulled his face to mine. Then I kissed him hard and long. We dove deep into one another, then ventured deeper. When I pulled away and pressed my head to his bare chest, his heart beat steady in my ear.

There was no room on his couch for us until he bent down and swept everything off with one arm. I laughed as the ziplock bags, the tinfoil, the piles of books, newspapers, and rolling papers tumbled to the floor. I stepped gingerly around the clutter and back into his arms. Our mouths met again, hungry, desperate, and my knees began to tremble. This was what mouths were for.

He sat down on the couch and pulled me into his lap. His mustardy, smoky smell invaded my head, and I lost myself in it. In him. I wrapped my legs around his hard waist and held tight. This was where I belonged.

"Do you want to go up to my place?" I asked when he stopped kissing my mouth and began working his way down my neck. I was so wet. *So* wet.

"No. I'm not stopping this time. I'm never stopping again, Shea."

Sounded good to me. I climbed off his lap and slowly removed my cotton tee and nylon shorts. He smiled at my neon panties, leaning forward and pretending to lick them off me. I moved fully into his embrace, his tongue warm and prodding, urging me to the edge. *Right there. Yes, right there.*

I lifted his face from my crotch so I could ease off. Then I dropped to my knees and unzipped his jeans.

His penis was long and brown and absolutely beautiful. When I took it in my mouth, I was happy. He moaned and said my name over and over, which made me even happier.

After a minute or two, he pulled away. "I want to come inside you."

Not a problem. When I stood up to climb back on, he dropped onto his knees and slipped his hands inside my panties. He played with the lips of my vagina with two fingers, stroking me lightly, lightly. Suddenly, he yanked my underwear down to my knees. His fingers resumed their stroking.

Oh, my god. I closed my eyes. I hadn't come in way too long, but that unnecessary torture would soon be at an end. My legs shook when his tongue replaced his fingers and he began to suckle me. He swept his tongue inside me, circling, circling until I cried out with a gush of pleasure. This was a man who knew how to please a woman.

He stood up and held me tight for a moment while I savored my delicious orgasm. Then he lifted me into his arms and moved quickly across the room. He set me on my ass on the edge of the snack bar and spread my knees with one hand. I opened to him. I was so ready for this. *So* ready.

The angle of the snack bar was perfect, and he entered me easily with a groan of delight. I grabbed him around the neck and kissed his sweet mouth.

"I love you, you know," he said. "I've loved you for a long time."

"I didn't know. But I know that now. And I love you, too."

He eased his cock in and out of me for what seemed like the perfect amount of time, and we rocked together in that little kitchenette reeking of pot brownies and sex. My sex. *Our* sex.

When he came, his deep shudder rocked me enough so that I came again, too.

Wow, oh wow, we were good together.

We held on to one another, our sweaty chests, our damp hair, our deep breaths melding together. "No wonder they call you Heaven Scent," he whispered in my ear. "Heaven s-e-n-t," he added.

I laughed. "From now on, this chick is Shea O'Grady. Hope she's good enough."

"More than enough." Then he kissed me again.

****

While Buck got everything in place, I took care of the Mini. I went to my guys at the garage on the corner of Pershing and Centre. They loved servicing my antique vehicle and got a kick out of running it up and down the side streets of JP, so they always treated me fairly. The head mechanic promised me the new battery would be installed by closing time and I could pick up the car at five.

When I got back to my place, the girls were in the living room with Mary-Ann, who had dropped by to hear how the previous evening turned out. After we'd finished showing her the goods and detailing the night's sordid events, I explained my plans for the hours to come. To my delight, everyone hopped on board.

"So this will be our diva girl group's very last song? Tell me it's not so. But hell, I want to help out,"

Mary-Ann said. "Kyle's with the kids so I can stay for a while."

"We screw the screwer. Has a real good melody to it," Skipper added with a grin. "I hate pimps anyway. Women ought to work for other women in the whore business. Women would do one another justice. We'd take care of each other, even when we're selling ourselves as commodities."

"Oh, yeah. So let's blow that fucker up," Ginger added with a toss of her flaming curls.

I laughed. After working things out with Buck, my mood had lightened significantly. Of course, the orgasms had helped, too. "Skipper's right, but there seem to be a lot more male pimps than female madams out there. At least on the lower rungs of the prostitution ladder. Like where I started out."

"Well, you're finishing at the top," Skipper concluded.

"And no thanks to that liar of a freeloader, your ex-handler." Ginger was setting up the tablet on the coffee table in the living room. "You going to wear the spy glasses again?"

I nodded. "We'll use the audio, too, record the whole conversation. As soon as I give you the signal, you guys send me the file. Shoot it over at once, and I'll show him on my phone."

"That ought to blow his trip. Jaysus." Mary-Ann laughed. Her face was pink with that love shine women get when they fall for a new man. I wondered if my own face had the glow.

On my way into the bedroom to change into some cheesy Heaven Scent garb, I stopped myself. Fuck that. No stiletto heels, no shorts up to the midnight line, no neon underwear. I would go as me, Shea O'Grady. Grad student, poor student. A smart girl with some stupid problems, a good heart, and a taste for the wild side. Not a hooker, though. Just a one-time cocksucker, a quick grifter who took some rude men, then took early retirement. A girl from the scrub who'd been dumb enough to play the game but smart enough to get out before it was too late.

Hopefully. That was the new plan, anyway.

If all went according to plan, Heaven Scent would soon be part of my past.

Chapter Fifteen

When I walked into the John Hancock Jazz Bar at ten p.m., the place was mobbed. Good for safety, bad for recording sound. I headed across the dimly lit room to his regular booth and, without waiting for an invitation, sat down across from Cedrick7Z. He had on a Midori green suede jacket, a peach silk shirt, and a purple paisley ascot. My eyes swam a bit behind my spy glasses when I looked at him. Jeez, was the man colorblind? I felt like I was having an acid flashback. The black gloves seemed totally overdone, ridiculous.

Cedrick7Z flashed his blindingly white and gold teeth in a wolfish smile. He'd snaked one arm around the narrow shoulders of a sweet looking girl with country-style freckles on her upturned nose. His leathered fingers made a stain on her virginal skin. I wondered whether he wore the gloves so he could manhandle his women without leaving his fingerprints. The thought made a bolus of bile hum up my gastric tract.

"I want a blue martini," I said, after swallowing carefully. "I need a stiff drink and I want you to buy it for me."

"Down, pussy," he barked. "I'm in the middle of a interview. Honey Pie, here, she from West Virginny."

I stared at Honey Pie. Her blue eyes round as buttons, the girl looked scared to death. Her tiny blonde pigtails shook like a kindergartener's on the first day of school.

"You might want to go over to the bar and get yourself a Shirley Temple," I told her. "This won't take long. And please send over the waiter with a Sapphire martini, okay?"

She nodded and scooted out of the booth. Her legs were like twigs. Once she dropped down out of her six-inch cork heels, the child wouldn't be more than five-two.

"Scouting girls from the local Brownie troops, Ced?"

He laughed. "You all full of you'sef tonight, baby. You score big-time last night? On my tip?"

"What tip?" I asked, my face blank as the soul of the man in front of me.

His smile hardened. "I tol' you to go hit up the professional basketball team in town last night. Stayin' at the Ritz. You didn't do what I ast you to?"

His frown deepened. I could have buried the looted coins in the creases across his forehead.

"Oh, I did all that." I smiled, adjusted the glasses on my nose, and looked him right in the eye. Man, his irises were dark. "We got us a few Rolexes, rings, and blings. Am I supposed to give you the stuff we stole right here, right now? I mean, what do you want me to do with all of it?"

"You move over next to me, Miss Fishpants. Slide it little by little across the seat here, lemme take a look what you got."

I sat right where I was. I didn't move. I was still smiling at Cedrick7Z when my martini arrived with absolutely perfect precision. I took a moment to thank the waiter, a rugged young blond with pink cheeks and a hot bod. He grinned and nodded. He probably wasn't used to friendly women in dress-down mode, and there I was in my holey white jeans and sloppy wife-beater tee, telling him how much I appreciated his punctuality.

"You make sure to tip the man good, Ced. Man works hard."

The waiter's grin widened, and he gave me a quick thumbs up and hurried away.

"I give him one a your hot Rolexes, you don't stop tellin' me what to do." His face twisted into a weird grin. Mean as he was, I could see he was feeling it. My badditude was getting to Cedrick7Z.

I pretended not to notice his growing frustration and sipped my martini. Delicious. I hadn't enjoyed a cocktail that luxurious since the last time I'd ordered one at the Jazz Bar. Only I never did get to drink that one.

This time would be different.

"What will you do with the hot items you had me steal from those ballplayers last night?" I asked. "I still haven't seen any money from the last gig you arranged. I'm feeling the need to seal a new verbal with my handler, see. So you don't cut me short."

"What you talkin' about, girl?" He flashed his grill. He thought he was regaining the upper hand. "What gig? Oh, you mean the crappy watch you stole last week? I got nuthin' for dat piece a shit. Your fourteen dolla drink be the only pull you get from dat."

My turn to heat up. Righteous anger flooded my bloodstream, pushing the gin ahead of it like a lawn mower to my heart. Muthafuckah was ripping us off. We took all the risks, he took all the profits. This was an even worse business arrangement than being his whore. The bastard. Buck had been so right. Cedrick7Z had a bad reputation for a good reason.

But I kept my chill. I finished my martini in one long, soothing swig. Then I said, "So who's this fence you bring the swag to? That watch was worth twenty-five, thirty grand. You settled for less? Are you stupid?"

He leaned forward and grabbed my wrist, squeezing until I cried out. *Ouch.* That wrenching grip of his would result in some nasty bruises. Again.

"My fence be my business. You go get what I tells you to get, and I pay you whatever da fuck I want." He'd spit in my direction twice while he told me off. His face was as wrinkled up as an old prune. "You get me, puss?"

With my free hand, I removed my glasses and dropped them in my lap. I said in a loud, clear voice, "Click and send."

He looked puzzled. "The fuck you talkin' about? Click and send what?"

I smiled. "You're outmoded, Ced, and you don't even know it. You're still living in the Dark Ages of whoring. These days, the best managers use an app to market their girls. A website with servers overseas, where it's legal. The best girls, they work their brands. They're savvy with social networking and search engine optimization. They forgo the sleazy pimp for a manager to do all their bookings, health screenings, background checks. Prostitution is a multibillion dollar a year profession in this country, Ced. And Boston is one of the highest paying locations. A sex worker with smarts in this city can make a very good living, pulling in an average of four hundred dollars an hour. And she sure don't need a scumbag pimp like you taking a greedy bite of her pie."

When his grip tightened, I pulled my arm, trying to get loose. His eyes narrowed. A wolf sensing a trap.

My phone rang. "Sorry, man, I got to take this. It's about the swag."

Wary now, he let go of my wrist, and I cradled it for a second with my other hand. If he'd been holding my neck, I'd be dead now. He had a grip like some fancy-ass power tool. Fucking ouch.

For a minute, I pecked at the disposable phone I'd picked up earlier while I was waiting for my car battery to be replaced. I turned the volume up as far as it would go, hoping the bar background noise, the jazz trio, the happy drinkers and music lovers had not completely overwhelmed the audio.

After I clicked open the file, I propped the phone between us on the linen tablecloth. "Check this out, Ced," I said as the recording I'd made with my spy glasses began to play.

"I want a blue martini. I need a stiff drink, and I want you to buy it for me."

I sounded cool, impressively assertive.

"Down, pussy. I'm in the middle of a interview. Honey Pie, here, she from West Virginny."

Even his recorded voice sounded dangerous, as threatening and as low to the ground as a desert rattler.

"What the fuck?" Before I could stop him, Cedrick7Z grabbed the phone and dunked it in his martini. "You stupid bitch."

I snatched up my glasses and put them on. Boy, was I glad I'd finished my own delightful drink. He'd just put to waste some mighty fine gin.

Jumping to my feet before he could grab my wrist and twist, I hopped out of the booth. Then I backed up a few steps and turned to wave at my friend, the cute waiter. As he hurried over to our booth, I leaned down and, with one finger, flicked the two gold hoops in Ced's ear. Then I spoke into the other ear. "The file came from an investigative journalist for the website Tell All. They have fifty million viewers a month."

A slight exaggeration, but I was talking to a grade A liar. So do as they do, right?

"Men and women need to play on the same team for both parties to win," I scolded. "I gave you a chance and you fucked it up. Now I'm going solo. Anything happens to me or to anyone I care about, that sweet little story is front page news. Got it, stupid-bitch-baby-puss-fishpants-pussycake-peckerwood?"

My waiter arrived, punctual as always. He stood beside me, smiling, innocent in his youthful willingness to serve others for low pay. "Another round, folks?" His pink face registered shock when he noticed the cell phone in the martini glass. "Oh, dear. I'll be right back with a fresh drink for you, sir."

"He's done for the night," I said. "But I'll have another martini. You can add it to *his* tab."

As I walked away with my waiter, I gave old Cedrick7Z a queeny wave. His face was the color of eggplants before you fry them in a hot skillet with tomato sauce and Parmesan cheese. If I'd still had my phone, I would have taken a picture.

Oh, that's right. I had my spy glasses on. All the photos I'd need—and all the video and audio—were already on file. I could access that in my email account.

And my crew was sitting in my living room, laughing and watching the fun. And sending copies to themselves.

So, yeah, I was all set. Thanks to Antoine's high-tech loaner, we now had on file a visual and oral record of the final meeting with my former handler.

"I think it's a wrap," I said under my breath to the crew. And, if I said so myself, I thought I'd handled the situation quite well.

The ultimate blow off. A huge success.

"Excuse me?" my waiter asked.

He leaned against the bar, smiling at me, his serving tray tucked under one long arm. What a cutie. If I hadn't so recently committed myself to a wonderful man, I would have been tempted to give blondie my number.

Instead, I told him to cancel my drink order. Then I handed him a fifty dollar bill. "I wouldn't go back to that table again tonight if I were you. I just broke up with him. And he's kind of a bad sport."

My waiter patted me on the shoulder. "Good for you. You can do much better than a creep like that."

We smiled at one another. Then I walked out of there as Marilyn Monroe-ishly as I could in my battered sneakers. And a pair of black-framed glasses that recorded everything I saw and heard.

Jane Bond, anyone? You can call me Double 07.

Double 07Z.

****

Since my phone was in the drink, I used the spy glasses to talk to my crew. I asked the girls to call Buck and tell him to pick me up at the prearranged spot.

The night was refreshingly cool. I walked the few

blocks to the meeting place, enjoying the rush of traffic, the bleep of horns, the distant sirens and occasional drunken yells. I basked in the sounds of the city.

My city.

A few minutes later, my knight in Rastafarian armor rode up and rescued me. When I spotted the dented Honda from the front steps of the Boston Public Library, I had a tiny orgasm. I was so into that man. Wow.

Before I made it all the way down the steps and into my waiting chariot, though, a man's voice leaped out of the shadows at the base of the darkened building. "Shea?"

I jumped. A kid in a white hoodie rode a mountain bike out of the darkness. "How'd it go?" he asked, skidding to a stop at the bottom of the stairs.

I said fine, hurried the rest of the way down, and handed him the glasses.

"You need something else from us?"

"I need to talk to Bunny again. Then I'll return the rest of your equipment. Shit is awesome."

The kid grinned. "Sure is. That's what made me want to be a blogger. I never was much of a writer, and I dropped out of college a few years ago. But I love techie spyware." He pocketed the glasses, met my eyes. "Couldn't believe my luck when I got this gofer job working for Tell All. They gave me a chance. And once the Australian mess is cleared up, they're gonna promote me to staff writer."

"Cool." I couldn't believe he was over eighteen. Was I that old? But I loved his enthusiasm.

After he got hold of Antoine, he passed me his phone. I walked toward the street where Buck sat waiting for me in his car. I wanted him to hear what I had to say to my ex-boyfriend.

"Bun, I want you to know that I never really loved you." Might as well dive right in the deep end, get the cold shock over with. "See, I didn't know who you were. And, worse than that, I didn't know who *I* was." When Antoine started to interrupt, I said, "Please. Just let me get through this. It's hard."

He said okay.

Buck got out of the Honda and stood in front of me, listening, his head cocked to one side. The moonlight dappled his skin, sparking it here and there, making him look like he was covered with mica. The highlights in his hair were almost as bright as the stars peeking through the night clouds overhead.

"When you left me like that, I was crushed. I blamed myself. I lost my self-worth. I went down to the dirt and wallowed there. I made bad choices, did stupid things. And I blamed you. But you're not at fault. I get that now. You have a passion for what you do, and I admire that. I wish you much success, and I'm sure that, because of your devotion to your work, success will be yours."

I wasn't crying. Not even close. I felt unburdened. I felt like I'd admitted the truth to myself, as well as Antoine. And Buck. Who was looking into my eyes like he cared. Which, I realized, he did. He really did.

"You ready to return my equipment now, Sugarbear?" Antoine, always one for deep communication and understanding. "You can give it to the kid."

"I'm keeping the tablet. It's handy. By the way, what is *the kid's* name? Am I allowed to know?" I was tired of misleading aliases. "And if you want him to be able to function properly, you ought to give *him* the Mini. That bike of his is better for peddling marijuana." Buck frowned, so I touched his arm, mouthed *sorry*. "And the white hoodie has to go. He stands out in that thing. You can see him coming some two hundred yards off. Be a dude and buy him some decent clothes. He's a good...man."

"I don't think I've ever heard you sound so...so bossy," Antoine managed to say before I cut him off.

"See you around the blogosphere," I said and hung up.

Then I grabbed Buck and kissed him hard on the mouth. "I love you, Rascal Bearman," I said right into his handsome face.

He kissed me back with as much gusto as I'd ever needed. Enough to make me love somebody long and hard.

I walked over to the kid and handed him the phone. And the keys to my apartment. And the keys to Buck's. And the keys to Antoine's car.

"The Mini is parked on the Jamaica Way near Pershing. It has a new battery. Sometimes it slips in second gear, but it's a blast to drive. You'll love it. Please take care of Antoine's apartment until he gets back. He has a wicked nice entertainment center. All that other shit is mine. Use it or sell it, do whatever you want."

He looked at me like I was a madwoman, which I was.

"Buck's place needs to be cleaned up. Can you do that?"

He nodded, his mouth hanging open. He must have

felt like he'd fallen into a dream.

"Once that's done, you might want to apply for the building manager's job. Buck is resigning, so there'll be an immediate opening. Not a bad job, and you get the apartment for free. Might work for you. That's if you decide to stay there. In Jamaica Plain."

He nodded again, at a loss for words. Who wouldn't be? I was giving him a new life. He could have our old lives. We were off to make new ones ourselves.

"What's your name?" I asked him.

"Thad," he whispered. "Name's Thadius Mayhew Dreyfus."

I held out my hand, and he shook it. His grip was firm.

"I'll watch for your byline, Thadius Mayhew Dreyfus. I'll be looking forward to reading what you have to say."

Buck was waiting in the car. I got in, and we eased into the flow of Saturday night traffic. Arlington Street was more clogged than a sink drain full of bran. So I negotiated with Buck until he capitulated, and we shot out the Mass Pike.

As we scooted down the turnpike, I called Freeman Dorff to cancel our upcoming tutoring session. And all those scheduled to follow. He was cool with that.

"Please apologize to your mother," I told him.

"Now maybe she'll let me apply to the college *I* want to attend," Freeman said.

"Where's that?"

"Seattle Hills Community. They have an awesome skateboard park there."

I wished my last student good luck, then hung up.

Buck and I, we were disappearing. Poof.

As we sped past the exit for Newton, I leaned over to kiss my man's smooth cheek. "How's the secret compartment in your trunk, babe? Weighted down with all our jewels and cash?"

Buck laughed. "The load's a little heavy, and this rattletrap's not used to hauling anything heavier than brownie pans of homebaked. But it's okay. It's safe. Until we get wherever it is we're going. Got any ideas?"

I snuggled a little. Yum, he smelled sweet 'n' spicy tonight. "I'm thinking we might start off in north Florida. See my mom, then keep on heading south to the Keys. You ever want to live on an island?"

Buck was silent, brooding. I licked his ear. Tasted just like I thought it would. I wanted the whole hickory pie.

"I know a guy who knows a guy in Miami," Buck said. "We might want to stop off there, too. Sell off some of our stuff."

We would need to get over to I-95, so I pulled up the appropriate maps on the tablet Buck had stashed in the glove compartment. "Sounds like a plan."

Later, when we were on our way south, I leaned over to my honey and whispered, "I think we'll look mighty fine with buzz cuts in a whiter shade of pale, Bucko."

When he shook his head, his precious dreads tossed themselves about in protest. "Not down with that, darlin'."

"Promise I'll love you no matter what kind of weird you look like," I told him.

But Buck wasn't into my makeover plans. He

thought I was being paranoid. However, we'd both agreed it was the perfect time for us to make some life changes. Quit our underground jobs. Get outta town. Go walkabout. And we planned to be undercover for a while. At least until we were sure Cedrick7Z and the basketball player and the lawyer from Malden and the cops and the DA's office weren't looking for a sleazy girl who looked a lot like me and a handsome pot dealer who looked a lot like Buck.

"I love you, too, Shea O'Grady," he said to me.

We stared at one another. The man had the most genuine smile I ever saw.

I was pumped. Because the coolest thing was, I believed him.

Epilogue

Almost Three Years Later

When Skipper called, I was sitting on the front porch with my tablet, reading a dynamite article. All about the intricacies of the dark Web, anonymity software, and online black market pharmacies. The in-depth piece was written by a reporter who had gone undercover to work in the secret office of the most notorious owner of a billion dollar online drug site. An investigative journalist named Thadius Mayhew Dreyfus.

As soon as I picked up, she started in. Again.

"You guys coming or not? Because I need to know. Now, today. This is a freaking formal occasion, girlfriend. You can't just stroll into the Ritz Carlton like some streetwalker or something. You gotta have your name in a fancy font embossed on a little white card that sits in front of a bone china plate. A plate placed just so on starched white linen. At a big table in a big ballroom, a front row and center table selected especially for you."

"You're stressing me out, Skip. Oh, god, I feel pressured," I joked. "It must be difficult emotionally for you, too, though. Forcing your sleazy pals to dress like highbrows and hobnob with a bunch of black tie types. Imagine, the seduce and rob gang making nice with the upper crust at your wildly overpriced wedding."

She laughed. "Oh, you have no idea the stress I'm under. This foolish event is scheduled for the weekend before finals. What was I thinking? If I don't pass pharmacology, I am fucked in the ass."

"Nice talk for a bride to be. Are you blushing? Cuz you should be."

She snorted. "Denver likes it when I talk dirty. I do have to watch my mouth around his parents, though. They already think I'm a bit of a mutt. Compared to their purebred crowd. And I gotta watch my mouth around my own folks, too. Daddy's little girl can't be trash talkin' like a state trooper, now, can she?"

I wanted to go to the wedding. I wanted to meet Skipper's cool mom, her cop dad and his young wife, their little boy. I wanted to see Ginger and Mary-Ann, hang out with them and their loved ones. I had the money, I could find the time. But going back to Boston after running away like we had? The first year of laying low in Miami, adjusting to a new lifestyle as a South Floridian with too much sun, money, and time had changed me. The quiet life in St. Augustine and my teacher's assistant job in a local Montessori school had reshaped me even more. Things were different now. And I'd left my past behind. Way behind.

So how could I go back to Boston? The idea of facing my old, wild, unlawful self was simply too daunting.

"Ginger's bringing her latest flame. Remember the chick with the tattoos who worked at the Blackbird?"

"Right. That's like saying do I remember the lesbian who worked there. The chicks with dicks *all* have tatts at the Blackbird, Skip."

"Cute pixie blonde with the teeny rosebud on her cheek? No? She's a doll. Plays bass guitar in this awesome girl band. Anyway, Ginger lusted after her for months, finally won her over, and now they're together. Sabra's moving in here when I move out. I'm happy for Ginger. She's been awfully moody since Denver moved to Boston for medical school."

I didn't want to say the wrong thing. Like how maybe Ginger was in love with her or at least worshipping at the altar of Skipper. Like so many men—and women—before her. I wasn't about to lecture my dear friend on how she shouldn't have let Ginger move into her apartment after the girl finally grew a set and ditched her abusive boyfriend. Ginger was in recovery from unhealthy relationships; she was still healing. Skipper needed to tread lightly.

But who was I to judge and advise? I was almost twelve hundred miles away. What say did I have in their lives?

None. They were my long-distance friends now, not my posse.

"How's the business coming?" I asked, hoping to change the subject and thereby relieve my anxiety. The wedding invitation had been haunting me for months. I wished I could just make a decision and be done with it. "You have any interesting new clients?"

Skipper sighed. "It's so back burner right now, neither Ginger nor I are putting enough time and energy into it. That's another reason why I called, actually. To bug you about something else. In addition to my wedding, which is only five weeks away on June 6th. My upcoming wedding to which all RSVPs must be in by tonight at midnight. Hint fucking hint."

I groaned. She could be such a needler. She would make an excellent therapist. And a great nag of a wife.

"Hit me with your rhythm stick, partner," I said.

She laughed. "That's what I'm talking about, girlfriend. We want you to move home and run the business. Be crew leader again."

She paused, lining up her artillery. I braced myself for the heavy fire. I'd been expecting this. Dreading it, actually. Because the truth was, I wanted to move back to Jamaica Plain. I wanted to go into business with my old gang. I wanted to overcome my overwhelming fear. But I couldn't. Because I wasn't sure what I was afraid of. That I would suddenly slip into my former badass ways? Five minutes in Beantown, and I'd find myself dressed in hot pants and five-inch fuck-me shoes, scouring the Internet for rich johns? A vivid image of the attractive cougar I'd met at the Ritz bar flashed through my mind. I thought about that woman often and usually with a bit of a shiver. The kind of frisson you experience after you've slipped through an especially narrow crack to safety.

"What about Mary-Ann? Can't you get her to sign on?" I asked.

"She says as soon as little Kyle goes to preschool, she's up for it. Which is excellent. Love that girl. But we'll need somebody with leadership skills, Heaven."

Ugh. The job description had Shea O'Grady written all over it. In full-size graffiti scrawl.

"Kyle's buying out Centre Street Liquors, don't know if you heard about that. So they're pretty busy with that, too."

I sighed. I knew what was coming. No way to stop the roll of this set of loaded dice.

Skipper switched to a take-no-prisoners tone of voice. "I've done what I can to launch the business with Ginger, and we do have a bit of a local presence. But I've got to get my act together and start on my thesis. Plus put in the volunteer hours I need to get certified by the state to do counseling. So my time is gonna get more and more limited. Ginger's into it, but she's always at the café or hanging with the JP chicks. And you know Ginger, she likes to be told what to do."

We snickered. Ginger personified the word *crew*. And it became her, it really did.

Skipper's thoughts suddenly poured out in a wild rush. "Look, Heaven. I'm serious here. We need to capitalize on what we have to offer, and we need somebody who excels at helping us do that. Ginger and I don't even market our services right now. And neither of us is very good at organizing. Or future building. And this could be big if we do it right."

I knew where this was headed. It wasn't a money issue. Each month I sent everyone in my crew a nice slice of the pie. We were still working through the cash, had yet to move on to the bulk of the jewelry sales' profits. Which were excellent, because Buck's friend of a friend in Miami wasn't a scumbag like Cedrick7Z. He sold off the stuff, then gave us our fair share. Which was quite juicy and would last a good long while. So I knew the girls had adequate funding for their business, for marketing and equipment and everything else. That wasn't what was hanging them up.

"We can easily hire other women to do the leg work," Skipper said. "That isn't going to be a problem. There's a lot of chicks who need income in this city. And just think how easy it is to train people. We trained ourselves, no problem, right? But you're the one who put together the team. We fucking *need* you, Heaven. We were so good. We were the most awesome girl gang ever. It's just that we were in the wrong business."

Her voice had erupted into a rah-rah tone. Now she was cheerleading. I rolled my eyes. Sis boom bah.

"And the thing is, we could really change some lives. For the girls we hire, as well as the women who hire us. But we aren't gonna be able to do that unless *you* come back, Heaven. And help us run the game."

I wanted to say, yes, I'm on it, count me in. I really did. But what if Cedrick7Z was still around, and he found out I was back in town? What about Antoine, who had returned from his Down Under exile as something of a public figure and now had a whole floor in the Prudential building? What if he contacted me? What if...

"You got to stop letting your past determine your future," Skip continued, reading between my unspoken lines. "You have nothing to worry about. The big basketball dick won't be a problem. He never made a stink. Probably just filed an insurance claim and pretended he'd been robbed back in Springfield. So he shouldn't be a worry."

"Bum was scum. Glad he retired from b-ball so I can watch the NBA finals without barfing up my beers," I admitted.

I crossed my bare legs and looked down the front lawn. At the foot of the jasmine hedge, Mom was sitting in the plush grass, a big pink beach ball between her knees. She looked fantastic. Vibrant, healthy, happier than she'd ever been while I was growing up. She called out, "Get ready, sweetheart."

"Speaking of scum bums," Skipper said. "You see who announced he's running for DA? Yup, our favorite cheating lawyer. Oh, boy, I sure could make *his* scandal sheet longer." She quieted, let out a weighted sigh. "But you got to let sleeping dogs lie in their own damn poop. Besides, maybe one of his other bitches will crawl out to bite him in the ass. He's such a wiener."

"The Third for DA. I can see the signs now. He sure is a wiener dog. And you know what happens to wieners who run for political office?"

"They get caught with their hands down their pants?" she asked with a chuckle.

"They tweet themselves to death," I said. "But seriously, how does it feel to see his smarmy face on the front page of the *Globe*?"

Skipper's voice lowered. "It's like looking at a picture of myself in a Halloween costume. I kind of remember dressing up, but I don't recall how I felt in the outfit. Or what kind of stash I ended up with after the night was over." She waited for me to respond. When I didn't, she added, "I don't like to dwell on all that. Or fret about what my life was like before Denver. He's helped me accept my hang-ups and move past the biggest obstacles. Kind of like sex therapy."

She laughed. It was good to hear her so happy with a man. I'd had my doubts, but she seemed to be content in having made a serious commitment. And I did like Denver. Each time they visited, I appreciated him more. He was kind to her and attentive without acting like a sap. Plus, the guy was amazing himself. Tall, dark, handsome, brilliant, talented, and rich.

"Our previous lifestyle choices are over, girlfriend," she continued. "Sewer water under an old bridge. You need to come back north to understand you're beyond *your* old life, too. You're a responsible person now with commitments and restraints. Time to work on the dream. Get that doctorate in education. Running the new business won't be a fulltime gig. You could fit in some classes at Northeastern, too."

This wasn't the first time we'd been down this particular conversational path. But time had passed, life had moved on, and clichés aside, she was wearing down my resistance. I sucked in a lungful of humid Florida sea air and let it out real slow. I had to admit it, Skipper was the therapist—almost—and she was right. My dreams lingered, still haunting. Like a tease. Living in the city I loved, doing the work I'd always wanted to do. Hadn't that been the original plan? Before financial hardship, relationship depression, and questionable decision making had intervened?

Skipper kept at it with the hard sell. Blah, blah, blah. I fiddled with my tablet. Overhead, a flock of terns called to one another as they glided by in a cloudless sky. I wondered whether I would be as content, as fulfilled as I felt right that minute, if I went back to a life once so full of struggle and loss. A life warped by personal failure and debt. Not to mention bad blowjobs.

My daughter's giggles broke my reverie. I watched my toddler sit up straight. She bowed her tight little body, her full head of unruly auburn curls straining forward, like she was about to throw herself across the thick grass. Her round face serious, her little pink lips in a concentrated pout, my baby gave it her all. She rolled that beach ball right to her grandmother. Who did what any red-blooded American grandma would do. Cheered and blew kisses and acted the fool. I had to smile.

"My little bear's a genius," Della bragged to my husband as she sent the ball back to my daughter. "She's way ahead of where Shea was at this age. Shea still had colic at fourteen months."

"Screw you, Mom," I called out.

Buck threw his head back and laughed. His chestnut dreads shone in the late afternoon sun. His broad brown chest, the pecs tight and lovely as ever, glistened with sweat. He'd been working those delicious biceps, drumming in a world music band. Loved that sound, man, rich with the power to sweep me up, take me somewhere good. But even more than the music, I loved seeing my man happy.

I felt my body heat up. Even from a hundred feet away, Buck made my heart put on fuck-me pumps and swivel its hips.

"Look, Heaven. Shea," my friend said in her most therapeutic voice. "Think of it this way. With our business, we're offering the women of Boston an excellent service, one so many are in desperate need of. We're the only all-female private investigation agency that specializes in domestic surveillance for relationship issues. Women looking out for other women. Just think, we'll catch those cheating men with their peckers in their hands. Save unlucky females from a future of repeated heartbreak. Get poor wives the severance, child support, and alimony they deserve. Women will be thrilled to hire us, and women will be thrilled to work for us. Women helping women all over Boston and the surrounding 'burbs. And you'll be helping out the city which has given you so much."

I snorted. "The city of Boston didn't *give* me

anything. I had to *earn* all those college credits, as well as the income required to live on my little patch of overpriced real estate. I worked hard. The jobs were dirty. Then, in the end, I helped myself to the goods. I took what I wanted. We all did."

"Maybe so, but you do have laundering issues. And Island Private Investigation, Inc., will offer you a solution to that pesky little problem. As well as a way to make amends, which is essential for your conscience. And your soul."

Soul shmoul. But the laundering idea, that was worth considering.

Buck waved to me and mouthed my second favorite three-word phrase, *Let's eat out.* After I nodded enthusiastically, he said to my mother, "You and Kent want to hit the beach for oysters and clams tonight?"

Della said sure, flashing my husband a wide, white-strip white smile. Old Mom was pretty foxy for her age. Could remaining hot, even when you're almost fifty, turn out to be inheritable, a genetic thing? I watched as she flirted with Buck—what woman could resist?—and wondered a little about the flirting gene. Maybe it was inborn, the seduction trait. Maybe it was natural. Maybe it wasn't all that temporary, either, because maybe the window for being an attractive sexual being was more expansive than I'd once thought.

"Don't be so neurotic, girlfriend. You never used to be so risk averse." Skipper had returned to needling me.

She was right, of course. But wait until she tied the knot and had a baby. These things changed a woman. Even a badass cocksucker could find herself a lot less jagged around the edges.

"Okay, I get your point," I told my persistent friend, cruising around on my tablet until I found the website for Denver and Denise. I would never be able to call Skipper "Denise." But I would try. At least, I would give it a shot while I was at the wedding. After that, who knew?

She was reeling off a complicated story about one of their new clients, a wealthy woman who lived in fancy schmancy Lexington with a CEO-type husband who claimed he had a sex addiction.

"I think that's bullshit," I said. "He just wants an excuse to pursue sexual variety. Like all men."

"Well, there are different schools of thought on that. On addiction and brain neurology, non-monogamous sex and neurochemical release, all that. But the man is a true pig. He's all over the sugar daddy sites, scooping up desperate college girls saddled with school loans."

"Muthafuckahs. You know how that boils my blood. I don't know which pisses me off more, the college loan mafia or the wealthy horn-pops taking advantage of desperate coeds."

"You could be here doing your part to bring all those old billy goats to justice," she said. Half-joking, I hoped.

When I found the sign-up page, I entered my name and clicked on two guests, Buck and little Dell. While I was doing that, I said to Skipper, "Entrepreneurship is the new black. I know that, and really, I do get what you're saying. So maybe we'll talk about it next month. When I come up. For the fucking wedding."

Skipper let out a war whoop so loud my family all turned to look. The setting sun cast its peachy glow over the three of them, creating a tableau of familial paradise deserving of a two-page spread in *St. Augustine Magazine*. A gorgeous grandmother, her handsome son-in-law, and a beautiful baby. All dressed in white cotton. Shift, shorts, diaper. All three barefoot and sun-bronzed, relaxing together on a luxurious rug of lush green Bermuda grass. Playing together on a spring afternoon in a quiet neighborhood a block from the salty lust of the Atlantic Ocean.

"Mama," my daughter said, throwing her dimpled arms straight into the air. The bright pink ball sailed up and up, disappearing into a soft blue sky.

About the Author

Originally from Boston, Mickey J. Corrigan lives and writes and gets into trouble in South Florida, where the tropics provide a lush, steamy setting for noir and pulp. The Wild Rose Press is publishing her dark romance series, *The Hard Stuff.* Set in Dusky Beach, each novella in the series focuses on a tough woman in a tough situation who falls in love. Novels include *Sugar Babies*, a thriller, and *Songs of the Maniacs,* a neo-noir urban crime story.

Visit Mickey at:
http://www.mickeyjcorrigan.com

To chat with Mickey J. Corrigan and other Wild Rose Press authors of erotic romance, join us at www.groups.yahoo.com/group/thewildrosepress.

Thank you for purchasing this
publication of The Wild Rose Press, Inc.
If you enjoyed the story, we would appreciate
your letting others know by leaving a review.
For other wonderful stories, please visit our
on-line bookstore at www.wildrosepress.com.

For questions or more
information contact us at
info@thewildrosepress.com.

The Wild Rose Press, Inc.
www.thewildrosepress.com

Stay current with The Wild Rose Press, Inc.
Like us on Facebook
https://www.facebook.com/TheWildRosePress
And Follow us on Twitter
https://twitter.com/WildRosePress